Brett Farkas

Girl at
the Beach

A Sara Steinberg murder mystery

CHAPTER 1

The small orange life raft bobbed up and down in the middle of the vast sea. A distant crisp horizon line circumscribed them. Dried salt baked on their skin. The two women dressed in ball gowns sat under a frilly white lace umbrella.

"Pass me the moisturizer," said Barbara.

Sara picked up a small white plastic bottle and handed it to Barbara. Salt spray splashed across Sara's face.

"Champagne, please," said Sara. Barbara passed the bottle to the other side of the life raft. Barbara slowly rubbed moisturizer on her arms as Sara poured a glass of champagne, being careful not to spill it on her white ball gown.

"Any hor d'oeuvres left?" asked Barbara.

"I ate the last one," admitted Sara as she picked up a red high heel and used it to scoop up some water and bail out the raft.

"We have to talk about the banana pudding," said Barbara. A bowl of bright yellow banana pudding sat on a silver dessert tray in front of Sara and Barbara.

"That's our only evidence. His fingerprints are on it," replied Sara.

Barbara brushed her grey hair away from her eyes, "I just want to smell it," she said, leaning towards it.

"No, don't!"

Barbara's high heel punctured through the side of the raft as she leaned over. Air began spewing from the cushioning. Sara grabbed a fresh bottle of champagne and jammed the neck down into the hole.

"Don't shake the bottle, Sara. All that pressure..."

Air began whistling from the sides of the bottle and it suddenly erupted upwards with a trail of champagne behind it. As sunlight hit the sailing glass bottle it created a bright green beacon which spiraled high into the sky.

Water started bubbling into the raft and Sara began scooping with both of her high heels. Barbara picked up the banana pudding and held it safely above the blue water, using the opportunity to enjoy the sweet aroma.

The sound of coast guard helicopters could be heard approaching in the distance.

CHAPTER 2

A single girl at the beach, Sara Steinberg laid peacefully under the full sun, casually reclined in her favorite beach chair. Spread before her, the ocean was gently rising and subsiding, as if the sea was drawing in a deep breath and then exhaling.

Another mystery had been successfully resolved. There was nothing more relaxing than the time right after a case ended. It drew her to the beach with a deep familiar pull. It gave her a warm feeling inside that was complemented by the bright beach sunlight. Sara and Barbara had done it again. The great Sara Steinberg, solver of a thousand mysteries. Barbara had gotten most of the credit in the newspaper, which was fine by Sara. It was her turn anyways.

Sara ran her fingers through her black hair, which ran smoothly along either side of her face, and with the breeze enveloping her body she turned over the last page of the trashy beach novel she was savoring. "Hmm. That was an interesting ending," she thought to herself, "It's a shame she had to die like that, though." She left the book resting on her tan tummy while she continued passing the time in a warm reverie.

Sara relaxed, feeling entitled to laziness if it would only bring her peace of mind. Her ex-boyfriends were the furthest things from her mind, meaning that she was finally in her right mind. With nothing to worry about she found herself only concerned with carefree gentle thoughts, such as: "What is it about the seawater that gives my hair so much body? I should bottle this stuff and sell it across the country." And "Wouldn't it be nice," she thought to herself, "if everything was as free as the beach. You just spend time."

She felt so free that she was not even comparing herself to the other women on the beach. Not even the overly tan blonde girl whose bathing suit top and bottom didn't match by a long shot. At least she wasn't comparing herself to other women unfavorably, for once.

The ocean was clear and inviting, as evidenced by the empty beach chairs and wallets stuffed down into the toes of empty shoes. A toddler's bare feet wobbled across the hot sand, making their way to the softly lapping waves. Candy colored pails were left beside a half-finished sand castle. An array of picnic baskets were surveyed by a hovering flock of clever seagulls, patiently drifting on the whispering breeze. Two young men tossed a Frisbee back and forth, each one catching it and throwing it with a single hand. An old vagabond retiree absentmindedly swung his metal detector from side to side, slowly making his way down the beach in search of buried treasure, or merely some other way to pass the time.

Because Sara had found herself in such a good mood she naturally wanted someone to share it with. Her mind dreamily meandered over friends and relationships. In particular, she called to mind an old friend whom she had a recent falling out with. If there was anything that would break through bad blood it was a sunny disposition.

It had been two months since they last talked, or argued rather. Or screamed at each other, rather. But now all of that anger seemed as far away as a raincloud. This was a fine day for rebuilding bridges. The relationship had been unnecessarily disjointed. Joy was still in the dawn of her life and was still making the mistakes of an amateur at life. The situation was blown out of proportion. It was just over a man, anyway.

Sara took out her cell phone and looked through the listings in her address book until she came to the name Joy Turner. She was glad now that she hadn't deleted the name from her address book earlier. She pressed dial as she held the phone to her ear. Joy answered, "Hello?"

"Hi Joy, how have you been?"

The reply was exuberant, "I've never felt better!"

"So what have you been up to?"

Sara wasn't able to hear the response because at that moment several young bucks wearing short jogging shorts ran by and waved hello to her. As she tried to wave with the phone in her hand she lost her grip on the phone and it slipped loose onto the sand despite her lunging after it. As she scooped up the phone she could hear a sound coming from inside it that sounded like a rain shower on a small tin roof. She hurriedly said to Joy, "Sorry, I've got sand in my cell phone. Let me call you back."

She tried to shake the sand out of her cell phone. It sounded like a maraca. As she shook it back and forth it wriggled from her suntan-lotioned hand and fell to the ground again, getting even more sand into it. She shook her head. She picked up the phone off the hot sand, collected her thoughts, and hit the redial button. Joy answered immediately, "Hello?"

Sara was now ready to address the cause of their acrimony: fighting over a man. Sara didn't want the man for

5

herself, she just wanted him out of Joy's life, and Joy, on the other hand, wanted to give her life to him. After the shortest of courtships, she and Adam Bartlett were engaged. Sara had tried her best to convince Joy to delay the engagement, and afterwards Sara tried to have her extend the engagement.

"How are things with Bartlett?"

"We aren't together anymore. I haven't seen him in two weeks," said Joy.

"That's…" Terrific? Terrible? She didn't know whether she should offer congratulations or condolences.

"…interesting," said Sara, "I hope it wasn't anything I said," she added, a little bit insincerely.

"It didn't end well. I'm glad to have him out of my life," said Joy.

Unbeknownst to Sara, the old retired beachcomber with the metal detector stopped walking and took a step backwards. He laboriously stooped over and dug his fingers into the sand, feeling around until his fingers struck gold. He held up and examined a small ring. Mounted atop the golden ring a gleaming diamond refracted the sunlight into a burst of tiny shimmering rainbows. He slipped the ring into his pocket and hurriedly walked on.

"That's great," said Sara, "I was just worried about you, marrying him so soon. You hadn't even known him for a year."

"A lot of people didn't want to see us together."

"Barbara didn't mean any harm, she didn't want to see you rush into a big commitment and waste your youth on this guy."

"I'm thinking about leaving town. I've always wanted to see the Mediterranean."

"The Mediterranean?!" Sara was startled. Why would Joy run away from everyone the same moment she ran away from Bartlett? "You should come to the beach before you go," said

Sara.

"I don't feel like seeing anyone right now," replied Joy. What Joy probably needed right now was someone to validate her. She was in a delicate state. After making so many mistakes, now she just needed some gentle reassurance that she was doing the right thing.

"It would have been a lifeless marriage, trust me," said Sara, "For what it's worth, I think you made the right choice."

Sara expected to hear Joy affirming the assessment, but there was only silence. She assumed that Joy was silently nodding her head in agreement and was just choosing the perfect words of gratitude, but no words came as Sara listened and waited. Nothing, just dead silence. Something was wrong.

"Well aren't you going to say something?"

"I want you out of my life. Don't call me again."

The line clicked off and the cell phone read, 'call ended.'

She laid back in her chair, staring up at the sky. The girl who had only five minutes ago been peacefully soaking up the sunlight now sat stewing in turmoil replaying the conversation over and over in her head, her anger growing each time. A new world full of distractions began to take form. She began to have imaginary arguments with herself and began imagining herself in unlikely scenarios. After several nonexistent confrontations had run their course she resolved to be done with the entire situation. Why couldn't Joy just say thank you? That's fine, she would never talk to her again. If that's how she wanted to act, then fine. After all this time. She could absolutely kill her.

The background tempo of the beach was harshly broken by a child's high-pitched shriek. Frisbees and sand shovels fell to the ground. Sara found herself getting to her feet at once. She knew there must be something terrible beyond the child's cry. The entire mass of beachgoers began to stir. Whatever it was, the source of the commotion was nearby in the ocean.

Those that could see it were backing away, and those that could not were pushing closer. Sara stepped into the surf and slid past half-clad bodies until she made her way to the front of the crowd and saw the object of everyone's distress. Sara's eyes went wide, and chill bumps rose on her tan skin. In front of the silent crowd, floating gently on a bed of waves was the sea-swelled, badly decomposed corpse of Joy Turner.

CHAPTER 3

Reeling like a mad fisherman with a marlin on his line, Sara's mind spun around with ideas wrapping on top of each other, sticking together in tight braids, and against that deadlocked strain there was no sign of a quick resolution.

Puzzling it out piece by piece sent her head swimming, and drowning. The nightmarish enigma perplexed her as much as it disturbed her. Not since the disappearance of Ashleigh Bosley, and her subsequent reappearance, had Sara been so confounded. It felt like a surreal dream, a mad wonderland where time and space were topsy-turvy. She stood on the boardwalk brooding, deeply involved in the greatest of all human fascinations: a mystery.

She picked up her cell phone and held it for a moment, hesitating in the uncertainty of what would come next. She found Joy's number and hit the dial button. The phone rang. A policeman began to wrap crime scene tape in front of the boardwalk. The phone rang again.
As she watched a policeman taking pictures of her friend's limp body, Sara heard Joy's perky voice answer on the other

9

end of the phone. "Hi! This is Joy. I'm not here right now, please leave a message." Sara ended the call. The sound of scratching sand came from her cell phone again and it suddenly lost power. The screen on her phone was dark. She shook it twice and sand loudly rattled around inside.

Could the whole thing have actually been a hallucination, or a premonition? It felt that way, dream-like, like it couldn't possibly be real, but it was. She was talking to someone, but who? Someone posing as Joy, but why? Whoever it was, she sounded just like her, similar enough to fool Sara. Who would do this? There was a general dislike of Joy in some circles. She could rub people the wrong way at times. She was still young and making mistakes. She didn't have many friends but she didn't have a lot of enemies either. Not mortal enemies, anyways. It had to be someone close. Bartlett was cool and calculating, but didn't seem cold-blooded. Hot-blooded sounded more like him, trying to rush Joy to the alter. Maybe Joy had been keeping secrets, or keeping his secrets, trying to protect him.

Sara's line of thought was charting a rough course. Her confusion gave way to turmoil as she realized that she was the only one aware that something was awry. The policemen stood around the body looking it over, probably suspecting a routine drowning unless something jumped out at them, and Sara felt like jumping out at them, but the police station was only three blocks away, and she knew that this case was so strange there was only one policeman she could take it to. The right evidence wasn't that important in the beginning, getting to the right person was the most important thing. She didn't want to, but she didn't have much of a choice. That cursed detective. She wasn't happy about it in the least, but she was going to need his help. She took one last longing look a the crime-scene and then headed towards the police station.

She walked swiftly, thinking all the way. There wasn't

much to go on, but she had a hunch that Bartlett was involved. He must at least know something.

The station was even more subdued than usual. Her eyes had to adjust to the dim lighting. The bright pastel images of a sunny day shifted into dark shades of wood and iron cast in sharp shadow. The walls were cinder blocks painted over, and the paint had dulled with age, like some of the minds around here. The officers' desks had all been inherited from the previous generation. They weren't the only things that needed replacing; aside from a couple of the officers, the floors were thoroughly scuffed from the boots of prisoners and roughneck witnesses.

A man with long greasy brown hair and an angular face that hadn't been shaved in three days walked by in front of Sara with his hands behind his back. An officer followed behind him holding onto the chain of his handcuffs. The station was quiet as usual. Some familiar faces were sitting nonchalantly at their oak desks. Shawn, Penske, Smithson, Peters, Sara knew that she didn't want to waste her time with them. They were too straight and narrow. She needed someone tenacious who would go straight after Bartlett and not let go until he had the evidence he needed. She knew that if he was in this station he would not be at his desk. If he was working then that meant he was outside the station interviewing someone or ruminating on some bench trying to fit the pieces together, but if he was in this station that meant he was after some free coffee.

The police chief was standing over the desk of a young officer, giving some orders. She kept an eye on him as he methodically filled out the paperwork on his desk and she slipped by behind him without being noticed. The orders had something to do with his lunch for the day, "Make sure they don't use extra pickles." "Yes sir." Sara finally ducked around the corner and reached the door she was looking for.

There was a window into the room on the other side, she quickly glanced inside to make sure that her quarry was there, then opened the door that was labeled 'Break Room.' She found the detective she was looking for exactly where she expected him, sitting in the lounge looking over a crossword puzzle with a cup of black coffee in his hand. As her shadow fell over his puzzle, he swiveled slowly in his chair and looked up at her, "What do *you* want?"

"We need to talk. It's an emergency."

He said half-jokingly, "Are you sure you haven't been hypnotized again?"

He was referring to the time Sara had been hypnotized in a stage show, treating the audience to some of the most awkward pole-dancing since the invention of dance, and of the pole for that matter. Now that the so-called 'Mesmerist' was serving his life sentence for murder in the Bentham penitentiary, hypnotizing his cellmates and stealing their cigarettes no doubt, Sara decided to let the matter drop, though she did glance ruefully at the long cell bars standing outside.

Sara had already decided that she wouldn't mention the phone call. It would be easier to get this detective on the right track if she didn't tell him the entire story right away. She wanted him to do exactly what she wanted, so she would stick to the believable. The most important thing was to get him on the case.

"My friend Joy Turner's body was just found at the beach. I need you to start a murder investigation right now." The detective put down his crossword puzzle and looked her over. He could see the distress in her face, and hear the panic in her voice, but that didn't necessarily mean she was a valuable witness. "Her body was found in the ocean, you say?" He looked at her sideways. "Why would you think she was murdered and not drowned?"

"She probably was drowned, by someone else," she said,

"You should call in Bartlett, her fiancé, ask him some questions."

"Bartlett, huh. The real estate guy? Why him in particular?"

"I don't think they were getting along."

The detective quickly snapped back, "That means you have been talking with her. When was your last conversation?"

"Alright," she relented, reluctantly, "I talked to her today on the phone."

"Today?"

He called out to a veteran policeman passing by the break room, "What condition was the body in?"

"Yeah, she's been dead for days."

He paused to process this information. The detective began to relax as his excitement faded and his cynicism returned. He said to Sara, "You had a conversation with the deceased while she was underwater? Is your friend a mermaid?" His eyes darted from empty space to Sara, then back to empty space. "He's not here."

"Who?" asked Sara.

"We have a psychiatrist around here somewhere. Where's Stan?" he asked a passing officer, who replied, "Went down to the beach. I guess some kids saw the body, he wants to check on them."

"If they saw the body they won't be within a mile of the beach anymore." He pointed to Sara, "Tell him to come back here, look at her."

Sara still possessed enough patience to brush off his condescending attitude, but she was beginning to grow tired, and the image of her friend's body would intermittently flash into her memory, distracting her from her present situation.

A youthful looking officer appeared from around the corner. "We just got a call from a pawn shop. Some vagrant came in and pawned a wedding ring."

"Let's get on that."

The young officer then disappeared back behind the corner and detective Cole began to follow him.

"You of all people should know how important time is in these investigations," he said to Sara, who was following, "I don't have time to waste with you right now."

She followed detective Cole into another room. The young officer held out a phone in his hand and the detective picked it up. "Hello? Yes. Go on."

A greasy haired convict being led along by an officer lingered next to Sara and said to her, "You got a cigarette? Give me your number, I'll call you. Once, anyways." The officer behind him pushed him along. Sara ignored him. She said to the detective, "It's not him."

He said into the phone, "Can you hold on for a second?" then turned to Sara, "How would you know that?"

"He's just some guy that found the ring," she explained, "She wouldn't have been killed for just her ring."

"It could have been a robbery that didn't go as planned," replied detective Cole.

"A petty thief wouldn't go to the trouble of getting rid of a body. They would try to get far away and fast. The killer wouldn't sell the ring here, and he would probably tear the diamond out before he sold it, besides."

Detective Cole turned away from her and put the phone to his ear. "I need to follow up on this lead," he said. Impertinent in her exasperation, she snatched the phone from the detective and slammed it onto the receiver.

"I've got your lead," said Sara, "I was talking to her."

He did not move at first. The anger was obviously building in him until it forced him to move. He slowly turned around and said in a restrained tone, "Listen, Sara, I understand you've been a big help to the police force."

"So what-"

The detective interrupted loudly, "But I also know that you

have caused more headaches than most of the criminals in this town. If you have any more conversations with Joy, or if you see her around town, you give me a call and I'll check it out." "Well, I'm not leaving until you follow up on this, so something has to give."

Half an hour later, Sara clenched her fists and slung her elbows from side to side, struggling to slip free from her white straitjacket.

CHAPTER 4

The front door of the police station was flung open. The figure outside was at first cast in shadow by the bright summer sun, but it stepped into the mellow interior light and was suddenly flush with color. The bright silver hair on her head didn't convey age so much as it did sophistication, being expertly styled as it was. Her plump hips swung from side to side with each sassy strut as she moseyed into the station.

She carried her weight well, and carried a large leather purse at her side. The lines on her face told that she was normally very merry, as did the inviting smile that was currently on her face. She had a commanding presence, so girly and surly, self-assured. Her bright red heels hit the ground with the proud clop that would come from a trotting thoroughbred after its victory lap. She pulled these particular heels from her heel-closet out of sentimentality. These were her get-Sara-out-of-jail shoes.

The light green print dress she wore may as well have been a sheriff's uniform, and the twinkle in her eye had all the authority of a badge. She surveyed the officers staring back at her, inspecting her surroundings for any sign of insubordination. She was someone who, though not a judge, had spent plenty of time in the judge's chambers, and was an acute judge of human character. A grizzled veteran officer mumbled under his breath, "Not her again." He had recognized Barbara as soon as she walked in the door. He picked up the papers off his desk and got out of her way. She moseyed deeper into the station and approached an unsuspecting rookie-looking blond officer and grabbed his attention.

"Have you seen a girl in here, dark black hair, cute little thing, skinny, early thirties, but she looks like her twenties, and I'm guessing her voice may have risen a time or two, and there may have been some incident involving her being dragged across the room, does that ring any bells?"

"Steinberg?"

"Sara, exactly."

"We got her on disorderly conduct. We're holding her until she can get the medication she needs."

"Oh," said Barbara, relieved, "This won't be hard then. Let me see her." Barbara reached into her large leather purse and began digging around. She followed him down the hallway, all the while looking through her purse.

"I just didn't want her to hurt herself," said the young policeman, "She's obviously on drugs, behaving erratically." Barbara snapped back, "That girl's cleaner than my living room. Erratic, you said? You must have made her mad. We better get her out of there fast."

The officer stopped at a steel doorway. "She's in here. I'll let you say hello." Barbara sweetly put her hand on his shoulder. "I'll go ahead and take care of the bail, honey. Alright, let me see." Barbara swung her leather purse around to get a better angle and the officer backed up to avoid it. She reached deeper into her purse and shuffled random articles around until she was able to dig out her billfold. The policeman was waiting laconically until she pulled out a stack of one-hundred dollar bills. She counted out seven of the crisp bills and handed them over sweetly, "And here's an extra two-hundred for your kids to play with." The officer put his hand over the bills and slipped them into his back pocket. "That should do it," he said, "I'm sorry about all the trouble." "I know you don't know any better, honey," she said as she raised her hand and softly patted him on the cheek, "You can make it up to us next time."

The policeman jammed the key into the lock and then slid open the cell door. Barbara gazed down at Sara who was now laying on the floor, propped against the corner of the room, her black hair half covering her face. She looked up with the face of someone too tired to continue struggling. Barbara hated seeing Sara like this. "Bless your heart, you get into the biggest messes." In moments like this Sara was enormously grateful that she had someone like Barbara to struggle for her.

The straitjacket was stuffed into the hands of the officer as Sara and Barbara walked off. During her temporary incarceration Sara had come to terms with the insanity of her predicament.

"How much did it cost?" grumbled Sara.

"More than usual," said Barbara.

The police force wasn't going to be a willing partner. Sara knew the work would have to be done without their help. She would have to build the case herself, one that couldn't be as easily dismissed and discarded as she had been.

"I hope there's a good reason this time," said Barbara. Sara just kept walking.

Barbara opened the door for Sara as they stepped outside into the sunshine.

"Honey, your hair looks great."
"Seawater. I should bottle this stuff."

CHAPTER 5

Barbara was driving her beautiful grey Cadillac that shined like a mirror down the seaside highway. She knew better than to bring up the subject directly, that would only put Sara back into her jail cell mentality. She would wade into it gently, and let Sara reveal it on her own terms.

"You've been through quite a lot lately. I would tell you to talk to your rabbi if he wasn't in prison."

"I actually would go talk to him if I hadn't put him there." Sara continued staring out the open window at the passing pines.

"It seems like recently you've been spending all your time at the beach."

"Is that a bad place to spend my time?"

"Not all day every single day."

"It's an old family tradition. Haven't you read Exodus? Where they wander for forty years? I don't think they were lost in that desert, they just enjoyed the sunshine so much they took their time."

"Your tan is an improvement."

Sara appreciated the compliment, and appreciated that Barbara was giving her some breathing room. Besides that, she was relieved that she would finally be able to talk to someone who would completely believe her no matter how strange the story sounded.

"You remember Joy Turner?" she asked hesitantly.

"That little princess-" "Yeah, that's the one," interrupted Sara.

Sara meticulously explained the series of events and complete rationality behind being found in a straitjacket.

"Now, you're sure it was her voice?" Barbara added.

"The connection wasn't perfect but it sounded like her," said Sara.

"That's something…"

"Yeah, really."

"…that you might want to keep to yourself," said Barbara, finishing her thought, "I mean, seriously, keep a lid on it, against your better nature."

"Keep quiet? It's the only evidence we have. And the police, they're searching for a jewel thief instead of a murderer."

"Let them figure it out on their own. Not knowing anything might actually motivate them. Are you sure the voice wasn't similar to anyone we know?"

Sara was adamant, "It sounded exactly like her."

"Then this is some talented impostor we are dealing with. It could be anyone. Whoever she is, now she knows about you.

"Who in the world could it be? Everyone hated Joy. That's the problem. Remember that preacher? Everyone loved him. That was an easy one to solve. If her ex-boyfriends were in a lineup it would stretch around the block."

Sara thought back to Joy's proclivities. She had a talent for using men, but it didn't come naturally; it required a lot of practice. "But those guys don't want to kill her," said Sara, "they just want her to disappear."

"She had a wedding coming up. She was seeing blondie, what was his name?"

"Bartlett."

"The big shot real estate guy."

"Right," confirmed Sara.

"When was the wedding going to be?"

"A month," said Sara, recalling the invitation she had thrown away.

"How long were they together before they got engaged?"

"Less than a year."

Barbara shook her head, "That poor girl, she never could get her act together. She couldn't bear to be alone."

"This is the first time I've heard you be sympathetic towards her," said Sara.

"That was always the source of her troubles. She couldn't bear to be alone. Do you remember when she first moved into town? She was in a relationship in less than two weeks. The first guy that met her height requirement. A girl like that was bound to be unhappy sooner or later, and if not with Bartlett then with someone else. I tried to warn her. Something was wrong with their relationship, but I wouldn't say that it was entirely his fault, from the look of it."

"How was it not his fault?"

"Because of all of hers. That's why she couldn't bear to spend time with herself, because she was unbearable," said Barbara, and hastily added, "I'm sorry, I know you were fond of her."

"She wasn't all bad," said Sara, "it just looked that way because she fell in love with the wrong guy. It could happen to anyone, I guess. She was too good for him. But they both pretended that everything was ok because she was desperate, and he needed a trophy. It wouldn't have been a marriage so much as an arrangement."

"I don't know if she was too good for him, if they were together then they deserved each other. One thing I've learned is that people will always make mistakes when they are scared. I've never told you this, but one of the reasons why I respect you so much is because you don't make mistakes like that because you don't get scared like other girls."

Sara was sincerely flattered, "Thank you Barbara."

"You make some damn fool decisions, honey, but you don't make mistakes like that."

Sara was a little less flattered. Barbara, she supposed, never wanted her thinking too much of herself, for her own good. "I have a feeling that Bartlett is the one that did it. I had a bad feeling about him from the beginning."

"I heard he's a good salesman," said Barbara.

"I heard the devil sold his soul to *him,*" said Sara, "I already knew he was going to take her life from her. I knew she would eventually have regrets. I think she finally decided to stand up for herself and he was determined to take her life any way he could."

"That's the thing, he seems like a man that can get what he wants, why would he murder her?"

"You really think he's innocent? The man is diabolical. If he had done it then he would be the last one you would suspect. Since you think he's innocent he must be guilty."

A car honked at Barbara. She had been stopped at a red light and failed to notice that the light had turned green. She ran her hand through her silver hair.

"Bartlett couldn't have been imitating her voice," continued Barbara, "you would have known the difference right away."

"I don't know," said Sara, "It had to be a woman, but whoever she is I'm sure she's connected to Bartlett in some way. He's paying her, or having an affair with her." Barbara was taken aback by Sara's conviction, "What makes you think that he's a philandering murderer all of a sudden? Haven't you just not liked him from the beginning?"

Sara was plaintive, and admittedly unsure of herself, "I just think the man knows something."

"You just think? There's a lot of vagueness about this," said Barbara, "It's not like you. I just want to make sure that you're thinking smart."

"What are the three most important things in real estate?" asked Sara, "Location, location, location. He was close to her. It's a good place to start."

"Let's not start working on him too soon, like you did last time."

"We'll wait then," said Sara, relenting, "until after the funeral."

"Our funeral dresses don't stay in the closet for long nowadays, do they?"

"No," said Sara, "they do not."

"Let me know how it goes," said Barbara, "It's your turn anyway." Sara thought maybe that was part of the reason, but maybe Barbara didn't want to attend a funeral that she wouldn't be able to muster tears for.

Sara stared out the window again watching the old oak trees with their heavy bowed-over boughs passing by.

"I am thinking clearly, Barbara. There are many constants in nature. A man's heart is not one of them."

CHAPTER 6

The sanctuary was gargantuan. The Lord's house was a mansion. The funeral was held outside the church beside the cemetery. If it had been Joy's wedding Sara would not have shown up. She arrived at Joy's funeral just as the service began, hurrying and weaving past gravestones to arrive just in time.

At the last funeral Sara attended it had been raining softly, and the wind seemed to sing dirges with the fluttering leaves of swaying trees, the ambiance was funereal. Today the sun illuminated the day brightly and the sky was clear across the horizon. The weather seemed to be meant for a happier occasion.

The funeral was being held outside the old church that was to be the site of Joy's wedding. It appeared that the money that had been saved by the family to fund her wedding was now instead being used to stage her funeral.

The attendees had come to pay their respects not to the deceased, but to the parents of the deceased. The funeral was not attended by mourners, but consolers. If it had been Joy's wedding there would have been more tears. She was more pitied in death than she was loved in life. They didn't appreciate Joy the way Sara did, probably because they hadn't gotten to know her, including her family.

The thousands of dollars worth of flowers now lavishly decorated the grounds. Strings of white garlands were wrapped around a cedar arbor. A podium stood in front with red petals strewn on the grass around it. Arrangements of pink roses lined each row of seats and framed the audience.

Sara sat in one of the empty chairs on the back row. The attention of the consolers turned from the lavish decorations to the sound of hooves. Two beautiful white Clydesdale horses pulled an elegant antique wooden black wagon. The four foot tall wagon wheels spun with thin wooden spokes and iron framing. The horses clopped to the front of the assembled mass and came to a halt with a tug on the reins by the hearse stagecoach driver. Four strong gentlemen dressed in black suits hoisted the coffin from the wagon and solemnly carried it to its platform before the priest.

In front of the assembly the polished mahogany casket was laid out surrounded by blue candlesticks whose soft yellow flames flickered in the breeze.

The coffin brightly gleamed from reflected sunlight. It was dressed with cloud-like bunches of white blooms. The blossoms surrounded it and gave it a vivacious aura, as if it were full of life.

Her father gave her away, his voice quivering as he delivered the eulogy, which was entitled, 'The end of Joy.' Grief had cut deeper lines into his face. His normally befuddled tone of voice had become steely and resonant. After his emotional recounting of his dreams for her which would never come to be, he rejoined his wife in the crowd.

As the priest spoke in monotone, Sara looked around at the funeral attendees. Even with his back to her she could easily pick out Bartlett. He was the handsome broad-shouldered blond haired gentleman seated beside Joy's mother, his hand on her shoulder, leaning in towards her, he whispered in her ear, she nodded with solemn gratitude for the comfort he gave her. Sara then caught two eyes underneath a bald head looking back at her, Joy's father was not looking at the casket or the priest, he was staring straight at Sara. She quickly looked down at the ground, and when she glanced back up he was looking attentively at the priest as if nothing had happened.

Joy's father had given his nod of approval to Bartlett from the beginning. That may have been one reason why Joy fell for him. Joy's father had never liked Sara. She had been in the newspaper too many times to be considered a good influence. He would rather have his daughter living an unassuming life without real ambitions or achievements, things which he had no need of. The last thing he wanted was for his daughter to be caught up in Sara's escapades. Ironically, now Joy had become one of Sara's mysteries.

After the priest concluded his ceremonial words of comfort Bartlett released the hand of Mrs. Turner, then stood and held a bouquet of white roses in his hand. Head bowed, he approached the coffin as the mourners watched. As Sara's blood burned, Joy's mother was choked up with grief and let out a stifled gasp. Bartlett approached what was his bride-to-be and laid a bride's bouquet of white flowers beside her coffin.

His bright blond hair was crisply brushed to one side. A solemn frown was set in his strong jaw.
"She loved sunny days like today." He cleared his throat. "I only have a few things to say. We never got to know the bond of matrimony, but I consider myself a widower, because we were inseparable until death parted us. We were supposed to live the rest of our lives together," he faltered momentarily,

then his voice rose, "Someone took her from me. Knowing that is more than I can live with. I promise you I will find her murderer."

As she gazed at the casket framed by flowers Sara felt tears welling in her eyes. Bartlett's words barely registered, the sight of him standing next to Joy's coffin was almost too much to bear. Bartlett stepped away from the podium.

The mourners then filed out and headed towards the church to gather. As Sara left the ceremony she could hear Bartlett continuing to console the family with calls for revenge.

There was a large white sign standing at the graveyard's gateway, Sara hadn't noticed it as she rushed in. She regarded it for a moment, then she reached into her purse and pulled out her new cell phone. This one was sleek and black. She may have picked it out at the store because of her funereal mindset, but it wouldn't look bad with a little black dress either. She had avoided Barbara's advice of getting a bright pink one like hers.

"Hello?" asked Barbara.

"We're in business," said Sara.

"Why is that?"

"Because Bartlett is offering a one-hundred thousand dollar reward to whoever catches the killer."

CHAPTER 7

Sara was driving her old comfortable bright green car. Barbara had admonished her to get a new sporty car on multiple occasions, but the car had served her well during high-speed chases in the past. It was broken-in without being completely broken.

Sara turned into Barbara's neighborhood. Barbara's home was a quiet little beach cottage, a relic from the old days. She could afford a much larger house, and one nearer the ocean if she wanted it, but she preferred the comfort her home afforded. It was near the shore, not close enough to catch more than a longing glimpse of the ocean horizon, but close enough to take advantage of the salty breeze. The regal little house was covered with white wooden siding and light blue shutters. There was a small screened-in front porch and a faux grass welcome mat with a bright white and yellow plastic flower on it.

Sara could hear the roar of Barbara's vacuum cleaner in the living room. She rounded the corner to see Barbara rhythmically pushing and pulling the vacuum back and forth, cleaning any dust that may have accumulated in the past week. She swung the vacuum low under the coffee table, making sure to go over all the old vacuum lines in the carpet. The only upper body workout Barbara ever got was vacuuming or dusting. Barbara always said she had her best ideas while she vacuumed, it was like meditation for her. With the loud noise to invigorate her and the rhythmic movement to quicken the pulse, it kind of made sense. It wasn't Sara's idea of a fun time, and definitely not a meditative time. If Barbara wanted to, she had enough money to hire a permanent maid or butler, or both, to clean every corner and cater to every whim, but Barbara insisted that she liked it better this way, because she knew how to do things exactly right. Plus, the butler Barbara had hired that one time didn't exactly work out, although he was probably keeping his cell tidy these days.

Barbara was so entranced she didn't notice Sara's arrival. Sara stood at the threshold, knowing better than to step on the carpet. It was ironic that Barbara called it her living room, because no living being was allowed inside. That room was better attended to than most children. The pillows on the couch were placed at perfect forty-five degree angles. Purple fringe on the rug radiated outwards as if they had been combed, because in fact they had been meticulously combed. The ruffles on the lavender curtains were perfectly spaced. An antique cabinet displayed decorative dishes that portrayed proud calico cats in different poses. The small coffee table in front of the couch was covered with an intricately embroidered tablecloth with a white lace border.

"Barbara," Sara called out. The sound of the antique cleaning machine drowned out her voice. "Barbara!" Again Barbara didn't hear and kept vacuuming.

Sara finally took a step forward onto the carpet and Barbara's shocked face turned in her direction. She shut off the noisy vacuum, and as the motor whirred down she said,

"What are you doing stepping on my carpet?"

Sara took a step back, "Sorry."

Barbara locked the vacuum in its upright position. "So, what's your plan?"

"I'm going to arrange a meeting with him," said Sara.

"And do you think that he will show up?"

"That's the thing," said Sara, "I don't want him to know that when he shows up it's going to be me standing there."

"Oh, heavens. Why is that exactly?"

"He might not show up if he knows I'm on to him."

"Now Sara, is there some reason in particular why Bartlett would be reluctant to meet you?"

"I'm not sure exactly," said Sara, hesitating, "I may have called him a dumb blond at one point."

Barbara's suspicions were confirmed.

Sara reached into her purse and pulled out a thin real estate booklet. "I picked this up on the way over, it's got his number inside."

Barbara motioned for Sara to step forward, "Come on, let me see."

Sara was reluctant, as if it were a trap, "Are you sure?"

"Come on," said Barbara.

She took off her shoes, then stepped forward with trepidation and handed the booklet to Barbara. On the back of the booklet there was a prominent picture of Bartlett wearing a suit and wide phony smile, with his phone number printed below.

"That's fine," said Barbara, "A surprise attack. Where are you gonna meet him?"

Sara took the real estate booklet from Barbara and opened it to the right page, then laid it on the table, pointing to a picture of a quaint blue and white beach cottage. "Right here," said Sara, "909 Cherry street. You know, this carpet is pretty comfortable."

"Don't get used to it. Hand me the phone," said Barbara, "I'll set it up."

CHAPTER 8

Sara slowly drove by the seaside houses that were built atop sand dunes. Groves of twisted oaks separated each house. Sara counted down the mailbox numbers until she reached 909 Cherry street.

As she turned into the oyster shell driveway she did not find what she expected. She put her car in park and stepped outside. The address was right, but there was no house to be seen. She glanced back at the real estate booklet and then surveyed the terrain immediately around her. It looked exactly like the picture, with one exception: the house wasn't there. Sara held the picture up side by side with the vacant lot. Where the structure should have stood there was only a bare sand dune gently sloping down to the ocean below.

Just as she arrived at this realization she heard the revving of a car engine and turned around in time to see a bright red car that must have been Bartlett's driving away, because it looked like it cost as much as the phantom house. It sped off around the corner.

Her spirits sunk. She had ruined it. Maybe Barbara was

right, she was rushing into things. She had hoped that she would be able to elicit something from Bartlett that would help convince Barbara that Bartlett wasn't entirely innocent.

She didn't even have a chance to say a word. Just the fact that she was standing there must have told him everything that he needed to know. Sara wondered momentarily if he was actually smarter than she was, but only momentarily. He was afraid of her, at least she could establish that much.

The stiff ocean breeze blew Sara's hair across her face and she pushed it back behind her ear as she looked off in the direction in which Bartlett had fled. She looked back to the empty lot where the house was supposed to be standing. Slowly, and sullenly, she walked to the spot where the house should have stood. As she stared out at the ocean she wondered what she would say to Barbara. It didn't make much sense that Bartlett would be lying about a house in a real estate ad.

Sara became distracted as a fishing line flew out towards the horizon and plopped down past the breakers. Just down the beach a solitary man had cast out the line. Sara wondered if he might be able to shed some light on the ghost house. Maybe he had even seen Bartlett sneaking around, and would have some piece of information that Sara could tell Barbara.

As she walked down the beach and got closer to him, his figure became more defined. His biceps were perked up as he held the fishing pole suspended in the air, slowly reeling it in methodically so that the lure skimming through the water would somehow resemble a naïve minnow unaware of the gigantic trophy fish pursuing it. As he pulled in the empty lure yet again and reared back for another cast, he caught a glimpse of the girl above staring down at him. He swung his muscular arm forward like a major-league pitcher and sent the lure flying out toward the horizon. As he reeled the empty lure in and swung his sinewy arm back again he looked for the mysterious girl but she was gone. On the follow through of his next cast he noticed with a start that she had appeared right beside him.

"Are you from the insurance agency?" he asked. "What? I'm Sara." He had hazel eyes that stared straight through her. She brushed her hair behind her ear with her fingers.

"Oh, I thought you were someone else," he said, "I should have known. I can't get anyone to insure this place."

He had dusty brown hair and a strong jaw. She held up the real estate booklet in her hand. "I was looking for this house." He glanced at the picture with a knowing look in his eyes.

"What happened to it?" she asked.

He lowered his voice as if he was confiding something that shouldn't be overheard, "It vanished almost a month ago," he said, "Just disappeared," but he soon had a playful smirk on his face revealing his square white teeth and the dimples in his cheeks, "If you really want to see it you should have brought your bikini. The ocean took it." He was handsome, mysterious, and playful. Sara was intrigued.

"It's amazing," he continued, "anything that a man can build, the ocean can destroy in a moment. When a house falls in the ocean it just dissolves like a sugar cube in a glass of tea. Erosion has been eating away at this beach for the last year. That house was right on the edge of the tide and there was a small squall a month ago, it finished the job. But if you're really interested," he added "I managed to save a good bit of it. It's right over there." She followed his gaze to a beach house perched on the edge of the beach.

Unlike the other beach houses farther down the beach, which were built on strong stilts that held them safely aloft in the air, his home was built right on top of a sand dune. The house rested on a ten foot high cliff of sand that overlooked the ocean. Round telephone pilings had been driven into the sand, forming the stout braces of a barricade. It was built in a vertical line with the front wall of the house, and held back the thousands of pounds of sand that the house rested on. The deck was built level with the top of the barricade and reached over it, jutting outside the safety of the wall, but the overhang was supported by strong vertical beams. A walkway extended from the deck past the sand dunes to the front of the beach. Sara could tell that the walkway had originally been built with much more beach stretching out in front of it, but gradually the ocean had crept closer and closer. The house looked like a fortress built by a frontier warrior to keep out an army of hostile Indians. It was, in fact, a fortress to hold back the steady march of the ocean.

"He didn't fight for it like I did, that's why he lost it. Then I used the wreckage from his house to reinforce mine and made it stronger." Sara eyed all the worn beams that reinforced his sea wall.

"This house is a champ. It's been beaten for hours on end and it's still standing."

She tried to figure him out just by looking him over, but found it difficult. He looked like he had modeled his barricade fortress after himself. She couldn't even form a first impression.

"There's a tropical storm swirling around over the ocean right now. Fortunately it's going to miss us but I always have to keep my guard up. What's that saying about a house built on a sand foundation? I guess it's true after all. It's like watching the sand pour out of an hourglass."

He was all alone out here, but he didn't seem daunted at all. He must be possessed with an inner strength that reassured him he would be able to triumph.

"Here, take a look at this."

She followed his gaze downwards. Below the shimmering surface of the shallow water Sara could see some dark object on the ocean floor. Brad reached down into the saltwater and pulled out the mysterious dark object. He held in his had a glistening spiraled shell with several small spidery legs projecting from the opening.

"This is my favorite animal out here. The hermit crab. I can tell by the look on your face that you're skeptical. The hermit crab is the freest animal in the world. If it doesn't like its house it can move out and have a new one in a matter of minutes." "Hmm," Sara said as she thought to herself, 'don't hand it to me, don't hand it to me.'
He held out the crab to her as if it were a present. She stretched out her hand reluctantly, then when he released the crab she jerked her hand away and the crab splashed back into the ocean. When he smiled he looked like he was winking, she found it adorable.
"I wish I could be like him, but in the meantime I'm going to be like that guy over there." He gestured towards a dark brown crustacean that looked like it had been on the beach for some time. It's solid brown plated exoskeleton was shattered in places, its crooked legs were stiffly frozen in the air.
"The hideous dead one?" asked Sara.
"That ugly little thing is the oldest living species on planet Earth. They call it a horseshoe crab. The cockroach of the sea. It's at least three-hundred million years old. It saw the dinosaurs come and go. I think the reason the design is so perfect is that it plays defense, the entire thing is covered with armor."

Even if she still failed to find anything beautiful about the crab, she thought it was cute that he admired the sea creatures after living at the beach and becoming a sea creature himself.
"So you're building armor around your house like the crab, hoping it will last three-hundred million years." "Hoping," he said. "I'm Brad by the way."

"Sara."

"You told me that already. I want you to have dinner with me tonight."

A crooked smile crept across her face and her cheeks went flush.

"It's out there waiting for us in the ocean. I'll have to go get it." He nodded his head towards a large round styrofoam bobber thirty yards out undulating with the waves.

He pulled off his shirt and laid it at his feet. He had a lot more than inner strength. He had obviously been working hard fortifying his house, his body showed it. If his home was as strong as his torso, it should be able to withstand any storm. His abs were well defined when he merely exhaled.

She realized that she had allowed several moments to pass without responding to his suggestion. "Ok," she stammered. 'He must do sit ups,' she thought to herself. He turned and walked into the shallow surf. 'And lunges,' she added. He walked through the small breakers with purpose, then dove head first into the sea.

Usually one to keep her guard up around forward men, she found herself unusually relaxed. He had a deep confidence in his voice that intrigued her, this man who was wrestling their dinner from the grip of the ocean.

He swam out thirty yards over the deep water and grabbed hold of the rope that was fastened to the bobber, and slowly swam back using one strong arm and two powerful legs, dragging the evidently heavy crab trap the entire way. He gradually made it to the shallows and emerged from the ocean, his hair slicked back, water dripping off his biceps and running down the valleys of his defined muscles.

He proudly held up a cage full of angry blue crabs fighting each other, continuing their deep-sea brawl. An hour later those crabs were as pink as valentines.

CHAPTER 9

Brad pulled one of the crabs from the spicy boiling water with metal tongs and placed it on Sara's plate. The thick pink claws were evidence that this one had been a prizefighter. One by one Brad pulled out the rest of the hot dripping crabs and piled them on plates. He carried them over to the old oak table and sat beside Sara. The furniture in his house was rustic. The décor was nicely complemented by the dark wood floors. All in all, it was a perfect cabin by the sea. He served the boiled crab with corn on the cob and white wine.

"What did you do before you came to the beach?" she asked, before taking a bite of corn on the cob.

"I used to be a stockbroker in New York."

She felt that her market value was beginning to rise.

"Why did you stop?" she asked.

"I retired early. The lifestyle didn't suit me. I was good at it, but I don't miss it at all."

"That's strange," said Sara, "To not enjoy something that you are good at. I guess we don't get to choose our gifts though. It's too bad that I'm so gifted at getting into trouble, but then I enjoy it." "Oh, really? I'd like to hear all about that." She was relieved that she was beginning to be as intriguing as he was.

"Actually," he said, "I've been wanting to ask you, what brought you to that empty lot?"

Sara would rather not talk about her escapades, but went ahead and gave him part of the story so that it wouldn't exactly be a lie. "I was here to meet Adam Bartlett about buying that property but he didn't show up."

"Doesn't surprise me. I hate that guy."

"Why's that?" asked Sara, surprised that they had so much in common. She could tell by the strain in his voice that it was a sore point.

"I wanted him to help me sell this shipwreck a year ago, back when it looked like somebody's dream house, but he said he had more important things to do, he left me stranded out here. I even told him I wouldn't be able to afford the insurance much longer."

Sara thought to herself that the house did actually look like it could have been a massive shipwreck that was somehow converted into a house by a team of crafty sailors. And it didn't surprise Sara that Bartlett had enemies all over town, it was just like him to abandon Brad to survive against the elements on his own. It was exactly the same type of person that would callously and coldly murder his own fiancé. "I heard that he's giving a big speech at a real estate convention," said Brad with disgust.

"Really?"

"It has lowered my opinion of the business," he said.

The sun had settled beneath the horizon and darkness covered the windows. "Would you like some hot chocolate?"

"I would."

Brad gathered the dishes from the table and laid them in the sink, then gently boiled a pot of hot cocoa and milk on the stove. "So what was that about you being a troublemaker?" She relished the opportunity to tell him about her adventures, her current escapades excluded.

He poured the hot chocolate into two mugs and dropped a small marshmallow into each one. She settled in on his sturdy oak and leather couch, and propped her bare feet on the thick, weathered coffee table. "It used to be the deck of a shrimp boat, that coffee table. It washed up not that long ago."

He slid his arm around her hips and slid closer to her. Even though he touched her lightly she could feel every ounce of his strength. "Would you mind if I gave you a kiss?" "Let's not move too fast." As soon as she said it though, she regretted it, and wanted to touch his lips.

When she leaned against him she was immediately taken by him and nestled firmly in his arms. His warmth, burning in him like a hard-working furnace, radiated outwards and filled her entire body.

She began to pour her heart out. She told him about the time that she and Barbara had to escape from that island in the Caribbean, and the time she was almost bitten by a Tyrannosaurus Rex, or its skull anyways, its teeth were as sharp as they had ever been. She talked on and on about her eventful trip with Barbara in Europe, and about the time they were held hostage. She even told him about the time she was almost killed by the escaped convict.

Among the many good things about him was his ability to listen. Sara talked to him for hours, the conversation naturally blossoming out with every sentence. The way he listened to her, her voice must have sounded like a symphony. When he listened it felt like a hug. She had never met a man that would welcome every one of her thoughts like it was a house guest. The hours seemed like minutes. The ideas that she found amusing he found hilarious, and the stories she was nostalgic for he found deeply moving. The vainest notions she had about herself were not only well received, but resoundingly validated and heartily encouraged. The more he enjoyed her, she enjoyed herself. He made her love herself, and she thought to herself, 'I love him.'

CHAPTER 10

Sara knocked on the door briefly before letting herself into Barbara's house. She slipped off her shoes in a smooth familiar motion so as to not sully Barbara's pristine carpets. As she entered the kitchen, Barbara was seated at the table with a bowl of creamy yellow banana pudding. Seated across from her was a woman Sara had never seen before.

The shade of her skin was of rich dark coffee and she wore minimal makeup on her beautiful face. She was slender, with sleek curves. She was snugly fitted with a light purple garment that wrapped around her, from her cleavage to her curvy hips. She wore gold rings on four out of ten fingers. They didn't seem gaudy so much as fashionable in some foreign place.

Barbara was still swallowing her banana pudding, "Mmm. How did it go?"

"He took one look at me and drove off."

"That was fast. He's not going to let you anywhere near him now," said Barbara, taking another mouthful of creamy banana pudding. She then gestured to the woman to her left,

"Sara, this is a friend of mine."

"Nice to meet you," said Sara, being polite to the mysterious woman at the table.

"That's nice of you to say but you don't have to lie to me. You're a good liar though, I like that," the woman said with a wry smile that revealed generous gaps in her teeth. "Call me Mariana."

"Alright," said Sara, a bit embarrassed and searching for a way to extricate herself from the conversation, but Mariana was not through sizing her up. She stood up from the table. "You have an interesting face." She raised her hands to Sara's cheeks and looked into Sara's bewildered eyes, "You've got a whole world in there." She tilted Sara's head to the side and scrunched her face in her hands. "I feel a…whirlpool around you, everything is caught in it and…is swirling towards you. The voices around you are confused" She paused, lost in a sea of thought, then surfaced and added, "I could give you a full reading for thirty."

"No thanks."

She wondered if Mariana actually believed the things she was saying.

"Do you see any ghosts around me right now?" asked Sara.

"Not exactly ghosts," said Mariana, her voice settling into spooky and quizzical tones, "They are more like spirits, more…" She gestured with her hands in a wavy motion while she spoke, "more like the ocean." She closed her eyes and spoke slowly, "Sometimes if I look real hard…" Then she opened her eyes to stare at Sara, "I can see a treasure shimmering down below, that gold underneath the stormy waters. Even if it has been hidden down there for a long time, even if the coral has wrapped its fingers around it and the seaweed has grown over it like a garden, I can still find that treasure, even if I have to hold my breath and dive into the ocean after it." Mariana's voice trailed off and she became quiet.

"Something told me you were a treasure hunter alright," said Sara sarcastically.

"She's a spiritual sailor," commented Barbara dreamily, "That's beautiful."

More than being annoyed at this point, Sara was becoming angry that Barbara had been taken in by this psychic. Barbara of all people wasn't prone to being gullible, which made Sara even more concerned.

The prognosticator nodded with understanding, "You...would like to speak to Barbara alone, wouldn't you?" asked Mariana. "If you don't mind," Sara said. She led Barbara into the spare bedroom and closed the door behind them.

"A psychic?" Sara whispered forcefully, "You know those people are hucksters. The only thing they are good at predicting is whether or not you will hand over your money."

"This lady knows what she is doing," said Barbara. "She's crazy, bless her heart, but she knows what she is doing."

Sara could hear Mariana's muffled voice coming through the wall.

"Who's she talking to?" Sara asked. "She's probably asking a ghost what we're saying You would think there would be more to do in the afterlife than gossip, but I guess they don't have a lot to do."

"We've seen plenty of people like her before," said Sara, "and she's probably sincere. She thinks that she's helping people when she is actually leaving them worse off. Listen. If I ever want to know my fortune I'll just listen to myself. Whatever she's selling you, it's manufactured. Giving her all the money in the world won't buy you any peace of mind."

"I knew you were going to act like this," said Barbara, and she yelled to Mariana, "Didn't I tell you she would act like this?"

"You knew that I would know better? It sounds like she should be paying you," retorted Sara, "What does she tell you in these readings?"

"Well," said Barbara, "she takes a look at me, and we talk a little bit, and then she tells me what's going on in my life, and she lets me know if something's unbalanced."

"I'm guessing there is. You know she's just cold reading you and articulating the impression you make on her."

"I know that," replied Barbara sweetly, "That's how they all do it. More intuition than superstition. See, she thinks she's a psychic, but she's an intuitionist, and she's the best one out there, honey. She sees you right to the bone. I tell you what, I completely left my therapist. This lady does the same thing and better, for half the price. She picks up on emotions like a bulldog picks up a scent. If she wants to think that she's a psychic that is fine by me."

This made a little more sense to Sara, but she was still skeptical, "An intuitionist..."

"She knows you when she looks at you."

Sara considered this carefully, and a thought occurred to her. To have someone like this at her disposal, it was a funny idea, dangerous even.

"I wonder...maybe if..."

"Bartlett?"

"Do you think she would know for sure?"

"That's what she does. She's a professional."

"If she could get in his mind, she could help us prove it."

It wouldn't be the most dangerous thing they had done to solve a case, but it was one of the strangest.

Mariana called from the kitchen, "You're out of banana pudding."

"A professional," echoed Sara, "Then lets see what she can do."

Sara began to open the door, but Barbara stopped her before she could leave for the kitchen, "Now Sara, this isn't like we're hiring a caterer or something. This lady is a bit particular about how these conversations go. First of all, you have to say you believe in her abilities. She'll know that you're lying to her face, because she's that good, but she has to know you're making an honest effort. Secondly, whatever she suggests, you better go along with it because if it comes down to a vote the spirits are always going to side with her."

As they entered the room Mariana was in the midst of a conversation, "What? Child, no. Uh, huh. Ok, sure. Alright." It was the tone of voice that one would use with an old casual friend. As Mariana concluded the discussion she was left staring at empty space until she keenly turned her attention to Barbara and Sara.

Sara tried her best to muster up an impression of someone that was being sincere, "Were the, ah, spirits telling you anything interesting?"

"You can go ahead and tell me what you want, child," Mariana responded.

She was, Sara thought, talented. "We need you to do a reading on someone."

"Will it be cash or credit?"

"Definitely cash," said Barbara.

"It's a man, isn't it?" asked Mariana, "But what sort of man is he?"

Sara averted her gaze, but not before Mariana got a glance of her eyes.

"Nevermind," said Mariana, "I think I know the type."

"Could you give him a reading over the phone?" asked Sara.

"It depends. What kind of reading would it be?"

"What kind of readings are there?" Sara asked.

"Future, past, or present. Love, wealth, health, but that is not what you are looking for, you want to know about…guilt or innocence."

"I can get him on the phone for you today," Sara said.

"This one will be more difficult than most," Mariana replied,

"Sometimes the dark spirits, the murderous ones, they don't like to talk. They stay hushed up so they won't get caught. If I'm going to read him I can't do it at a distance. I need to be in the same room with him."

Sara couldn't believe how ridiculous the situation was, and how unnecessarily difficult the situation was going to be. The more complicated this would be the more likely it would be that things would go terribly wrong. It wasn't out of desperation so much as her respect for Barbara that she decided to go along with it. She recalled what Brad had mentioned to her at the beach, "Bartlett is going to be giving a speech at a real estate convention," she said.

The thought of Mariana wandering around the convention muttering to herself wasn't a pretty picture. "Barbara, do you have an old cell phone laying around here?" "I think so," said Barbara, and she rifled through a desk drawer full of junk until she retrieved the old phone, "Here it is."

Sara turned to Mariana, "Anytime you want to talk to a ghost," she said, "just hold this cell phone up to your ear and you can talk away without drawing attention to yourself."

"I'll get you a new one later on," said Barbara as she handed Mariana the old phone, "No, don't you worry," added Barbara, "I'll pay for it."

"She will have to look the part," Sara added.

Barbara looked over Mariana's mystical wardrobe from head to toe.

"You have a point there," said Barbara, "Mariana, I see some shopping in your future."

CHAPTER 11

The three shoppers passed by the quaint stores lining the promenade just one block away from the calm ocean. The old brick façades of the stores had been weathered by the salty sea spray for sixty years. Barbara walked in front, leading Sara and Mariana to one of the cute little businesses facing the beach. It was the one with yellow awnings and purple drapes inside framing the window displays, and pastel blue and green ball gowns trimmed with ribbon and lace hanging artfully inside as appealing lures for any ambitious socialite, young beauty pageant contestant, young beauty pageant contestant's overbearing mother, prom vixen, or even fortune teller. The sign above the door in bold blue letters read, "Beauty Queen Dress Shop." Arriving at the dress shop reminded Sara that she had agreed to be a bridesmaid at Joy's wedding, but that was before their falling out, of course. After that it was understood that Sara wouldn't be at the wedding. As Sara politely held the door open and the three entered the store, Mariana eyed the assorted outfits lining the walls and perkily hanging on racks. The blues, purples, reds, and whites were reflected in her eyes. Sara noted that this was probably the first shopping spree Mariana had received in her entire life.

Suzanne Stripling, the store owner and former beauty queen, was seated in the center of the store. She had eyes like those of a cat and sharply defined eyebrows above them. Her hair color of choice was bright blonde, her true hair color was a mystery to anyone who didn't know her in elementary school. Her lips were wide, pouty, and plump. Her smooth legs were only covered by a short blue fluffy miniskirt. Sara guessed that the dress Suzanne wore must have just been featured on a Paris runway, as she glanced down at her own pair of blue jeans. Suzanne always was a slave to the cutting edge of fashion. Her slender frame spoke volumes about her bulimia, one didn't have to be a psychic to ascertain that much about her private life. It wasn't something she wanted to do, Suzanne told herself, it was simply good for the business of fitting into the latest fashions. Her business model revolved around being a model herself. She must be a good businesswoman, Sara thought, because she definitely knows how to sell herself. Or sell out, anyways.

A myriad of beauty products lined the shelves along the walls, and were prominently displayed in the front window. Shampoos, face creams, cleansers, exfoliates, foundations, it looked like there were enough products to build a woman from scratch. And it looked like Suzanne used every one of them. She was in her mid-forties though she was striving to be mistaken for her twenties. She was formerly a beauty pageant queen, local royalty who carried out her short-lived reign parading prettily before her subjects until she was ultimately deposed by time, and exiled to live amongst the aging. Though she did manage to hold on to the crown itself, it was enshrined in a glass case by the cash register, its dainty faux diamonds gleamed regally.

On the far wall there was a blown-up black and white

poster of a perfume ad. It featured a girl in her early twenties that looked to be a young Suzanne striking a dramatic pose with the ocean filling the background. A handsome stranger with a stout jaw stood at her side, a five o'clock shadow and a dour expression on his face as he stared at her intensely. At the bottom of this smoldering scene were the words, "I look my best when you are looking at me. Diosno Perfume."

Sara's eyes moved from the poster back to Suzanne, who was flanked by a quartet of shop boys that worked with her. They each had meticulously styled hair, pin-striped dress shirts with crisp collars, and airily aloof demeanors, much like the mannequins they dressed. The lead shop boy, James was standing closest to her. He sported long eyelashes and was either blushing or wearing blush.

Barbara smiled as she approached Suzanne. "I like those heels, chic!" said Suzanne, rising from her chair, "You could poke a man's eyes out with those heels, I bet."

"If they wanted to look I wouldn't dare," replied Barbara as she turned one of the red heels to the side to show it off in profile.

Suzanne then surveyed Sara's ensemble.

"Sara, I would devastate you for wearing that outfit if you weren't so beautiful. It's so painful to criticize the beautiful. I can't bring myself to do it."

Suzanne then took a look at Sara's motley-styled companion.

"I don't think we've met…"

"Mariana."

"So Mariana, what do you do for a living?" asked Suzanne.

"Well, I just tell people the truth."

"I'm surprised you can find work. I only hire people that tell me what I want to hear. What sort of things do you tell them?"

Tugging on one of the rings on her fingers to make sure it was catching the light just right, Mariana replied, "Well, I listen to what the spirits tell me and then I just pass it along. It's not that simple, but that's what I do, and I could do it for you for a reasonable price." "We're just here for a dress," interrupted Sara.

"That's alright anyway," said Suzanne, "The spirits are probably jealous of me." James and the other men behind her laughed to themselves.

"You know what, I'm a bit of a psychic myself," said Suzanne, "I know that you are good people. I knew it as soon as you walked through the door. You know how I know that? Because this is the place you come to when you want positive attention. So, you want positive things in your life, that's the best you can ask for in a human being, that makes you good people." "I couldn't agree more," said James as he looked over into a mirror and adjusted his coif. Suzanne glanced back at James and then turned her attention back to Mariana, "I don't know if you know this about them," continued Suzanne, "but these two ladies have a reputation for stirring up trouble. They get away with it. It doesn't matter what you do as long as you look good doing it."

Barbara began rifling through dresses on a rack, trying to find just the right business costume for Mariana.

"Oh, Barbara, we can take care of that." "Oh, alright," said Barbara, conceding, "We want her to look professional, her very best."

"That's what we do best," said Suzanne.

The shop boys immediately dispersed in separate directions, each one sweeping a quadrant of the store with precision.

"What kind of occasion are you dressing for?" asked Suzanne.

"A formal one," said Sara.

"What kind of formal one?"

"It's just a get-together later on this evening," Sara answered back.

"A formal get-together, I'm surprised you didn't invite me,

because I was going to invite you to mine." Mariana surmised that Suzanne was in fact going to throw a party, but she had no intention of inviting Sara until the opportunity arose to spite Sara with her graciousness. It was probably, Mariana thought, the only circumstance in which Suzanne was gracious. The four shop boys returned simultaneously, each one slightly out of breath, though each one's hair was still perfectly in place. They all held two dresses in each hand and laid them on the counter. "Good boys. Now, let's see," Suzanne looked to Mariana and then turned back to the dresses, "This, this, this, and this," said Suzanne, pointing to the different dresses. James picked them up and handed them to Mariana. "Try those on," said Suzanne, "and we'll see how we did." Mariana stepped into the dressing room to slip on a dress.

"I'm having a little get-together of my own pretty soon," said Suzanne as she tilted her head towards James, "Everybody's going to be there, right boys?"

"Absolutely." "Yes, Ma'am." "Of course," "Everybody," they replied one after another.

"My last party was absolutely unforgettable."

"What you remember of it, anyways," said James.

"It would be a shame if you couldn't make it. You can bring your fortune teller friend if you want." "She's not exactly a friend," said Sara, "But I don't think she does party tricks anyways. Not for free, anyways."

"I wonder if she could predict what is going to be in fashion next year?"

Mariana stepped out of the dressing room wearing a mixed and matched purple and red outfit that clashed loudly. "Maybe not," said Suzanne, answering her own question.

"We have to fix that dress, thing, ensemble," said Barbara, "Whatever you have going on there."

"That's ok, I knew you didn't like it, child."

"I knew you'd understand, honey."

Mariana turned and walked back into the dressing room for another attempt.

"I don't know what exactly you are planning to do," said Suzanne, "but I want to make sure it looks good, because when her picture is on the front page of the newspaper I want people to know she got her dress here. Business has been slow, you know. Would you like to try something on, Sara?" asked Suzanne, "I'm surprised you didn't come in last week to try out some new funeral dresses. We have all the latest funeral couture."

"Oh, did you hear about the Turner girl?" asked Barbara, with interest.

"I just found out yesterday. I overheard some people talking about how tragic it was. I thought it was just awful until I realized they were talking about Joy Turner." Two of her shop boys giggled until she glanced in their direction with a wry smirk of approval, at which point they fell silent, having fulfilled their duty.

Suzanne was facing the dressing room, but looking at Sara and Barbara through the corner of her eye. "Why are you ladies staring at me?" asked Suzanne, turning to them, "You look like pageant judges. I can tell you want to ask me something."

"Oh, really?" said Sara, wanting to shift the discussion away from Joy as quickly as possible, so she obliged, "How do you keep your skin so smooth?"

"Drink plenty of the clear stuff everyday," she said as she lifted her water bottle.

"Vodka. It's full of vodka," said her dressing man James.

"Nice earrings," commented Barbara. The diamond earrings ostentatiously glittered in the light.

"Oh, you like them? They used to belong to Queen Victoria."

"Really?"

"Yes, really."

"That's what an English boyfriend told her," said James.

"It looks better with the crown on," said Suzanne, gesturing towards the beauty queen crown on display in the glass case, "but it messes up my hair, I'll spare you."

"Don't you think Sara's hair looks nice?" said Barbara as she leaned over to Suzanne. Sara looked down to the floor in embarrassment as Suzanne looked her over with the merciless eye of a beauty pageant judge. "Do a little turn or something," said Barbara.

Sara wasn't about to strut down a runway and put on one of those frozen pageant smiles. Not again anyways, that was years ago, best to forget about it. Suzanne's eyes traced the careless curls strewn across that black mane, they were as random and striking as waves on the sea. "That is glamour all over," gasped Suzanne, "Here, I want to see how this looks." Suzanne opened the glass case and carefully removed the beauty queen tiara. Sara stood frozen as Suzanne quickly placed it on her head.

"I've always felt that the fairest way to measure a woman's beauty is by her hair," remarked Barbara.

"I couldn't agree more," said Suzanne, "I have to have it." She tilted her head to the side, sizing up Sara's hair-do, "How much do you want for it?"

Sara looked back with a blank expression, "Want for what?"

"I'll get some scissors," piped up James.

"I'll get a bag," said another male assistant.

"No," said Sara, "I'll have to pass."

"That's a shame, but I was just wondering what her secret was," she said to her shop boys.

"It's nothing," said Sara, "just the ocean." Suzanne then walked up and removed the crown and carefully placed it on her own head.

"You dunked your hair in the ocean and it came out looking like that? It looks like it was styled by a mermaid," Suzanne nodded to her assistant James, "or a merman." "Thank you," said James.

"It's more of a misting," said Sara grudgingly.

The dressing room door opened and Mariana stepped forward looking like a veteran professional. She struck a natural and jaunty pose to show off her crisp khaki pants and a perfectly cut flowing purple dress shirt that highlighted her physique and complimented her dark skin. Mariana surveyed the three women staring at her and replied, "You don't have to say a word. This is the one."

Barbara slapped down a few hundred dollars on the counter, "That should do it." Mariana decided to wear her attire out of the store since it suited her so well.

Sara opened the door for Mariana and Barbara.

Suzanne called out, "Oh, Sara. Lovely hair."

Sara looked back at Suzanne, then walked out the door and let it close behind her.

They walked along the promenade with a sunny sky above them and a soft breeze around them, and Mariana now looking like the most respectable of the three. "That went well," said Barbara with an air of satisfaction, "It was interesting, that's for sure." Barbara then said casually, "Mariana, what was your read on the queen back there?"

Mariana replied, "The beauty queen? She's got secrets."

"Yes she does," said Barbara.

"You had something else up your sleeve," said Sara, feeling like she should have known that Barbara was on some clandestine mission, "What are you up to?"

Mariana closed her eyes in deep concentration, trying to peer into Suzanne's secrets, "I see her doing some nude modeling. She doesn't look half bad. But there's something more…hard to say."

"Did you ever see the beauty pageant that Suzanne was in?"

asked Barbara.

"I never saw it," said Sara, "I heard about it."

The story was that Suzanne had insulted one of the contestants at some point during the competition, and immediately after the coronation a hair-pulling brawl had erupted on the stage, though thankfully the crown survived intact.

"Did you hear about the talent portion of the pageant? Do you know what her talent was?"

"No…"

Sara waited and Barbara continued, "The girl did impressions. And as you might recall, she won."

CHAPTER 12

Now Barbara had her suspect and Sara had hers. Each one of them was rooting for their own. Sara wasn't even close to conceding a single point to Barbara.

"If Suzanne had something to do with it she was just being used by Bartlett. He is the only one who would do something like this." "We'll see," said Barbara, "Mariana will tell us everything." They were standing in Barbara's kitchen waiting for Mariana to fix her hair. Mariana promptly entered with her hair neatly combed in delicate waves. She noticed that Barbara was fixated on her shoes.

"You look like you're my size, darling," said Barbara, "I brought you a pair of heels out of my heel-closet."

"Oh, I couldn't," Mariana seemed to genuinely protest. Barbara handed her a pair of bright red heels, "I just bought these three months ago. You can have them. You positively can't go out there, or anywhere really, without a good pair of heels." Mariana slipped off her comfortable black loafers and awkwardly stepped into the red heels.

"How do I look?" she asked.

"Taller," said Sara.

Sara held up the small real estate pamphlet and pointed to an ad inside that featured a beaming white two-story home, and right beside it was a picture of Bartlett standing in a dark business suit, flashing his beaming white teeth, trying to force a welcoming smile. It always seemed eerie to see a picture of a mean businessman trying to act inviting.

"This is your quarry," said Sara. Mariana looked over the picture, sizing him up. "I don't know how easy it will be to get to him," Sara continued, "but do whatever it takes to get the spirits talking, or whatever, because he's on to me and we won't have another opportunity to get you close to him, and I feel like we might be running out of time."

Mariana opened her mouth with a grin, "Don't you worry, I'll get him. Barbara?"

"Yes, dear?"

"I was wondering if you could advance me some money?"

"Here we go," said Sara sarcastically.

"Here," said Barbara, handing her a couple of hundred dollar bills from her purse, "Just hang on to those."

Mariana tucked the money into her cleavage and walked out the front door. "She'll earn it," Barbara said to Sara. Barbara grabbed the keys to her Cadillac off the counter.

"You know," said Barbara, "If either one of us are seen there it could ruin the entire thing."

"I was about to say the same thing to you," replied Sara, "I wasn't going to go."

"You always involve yourself in the world, it's a habit of yours," said Barbara.

"Alright," said Sara, "I won't go, but only if you don't go either."

"Agreed."

CHAPTER 13

Outside the convention building, Sara snuck around back to find a window that would provide a good view for someone surreptitiously watching the proceedings. She understood the intentions behind what Barbara had said, but sometimes Barbara didn't seem to understand the importance of involving oneself in any situation, as long as it is in reach. Sara reminded herself that even though she had learned a lot from Barbara, she still had an independent streak that couldn't be ignored and rarely led her astray. She held her head high as she passed by a handsome real estate salesman in a sharp business suit with a manila folder tucked under his arm. Sara stared straight ahead to avoid eye contact and hopefully become as forgettable as possible. This was not a natural approach for her to take. She knew that she had a way of immortalizing herself; the right glance can be unforgettable.

She successfully passed the businessman and began scouting out a good spying position. Most of the windows were obscured by tall decorative bushes. At least they would make for good cover. She picked out a prickly bush that covered a window with a prime position. As she moved closer, Sara noticed someone crouching behind the bush. The person wasn't moving, obviously trying not to be seen, which meant they had seen Sara. She suddenly regretted coming to this event, and she recognized the risk of ruining whatever chance Mariana would have of uncovering the truth. A whisper shot out from behind the bush, "Sara, come here."

A face peeked out. It was Barbara's. Sara walked around the prickly bush and said, "Why are you here?"
"I wanted to make sure she didn't mess this up," said Barbara, "Why are you here?"
"I wanted to watch her mess this up. At least one of us won't be disappointed."

They were both safely obscured by the landscaping. Barbara turned and looked through the window. "I've got a pretty good view from here."

Sara looked for herself. She was glad to have Barbara's company. At least she could outrun her if something went wrong.

The salesmen were dressed in crisp business suits, the women in professional dresses not unlike Mariana's. "There she is," said Barbara.

In the back of the room Mariana made her unassuming entrance. The evening sun glinted off of her two golden hoop earrings, which complimented the purple dress shirt. She blended in well, except she looked bewildered, unsure where to start. Sara realized that she had neglected to go over the finer points of small talk during their preparation. "She doesn't look too good," said Sara. "This was your idea," replied Barbara.

The businessmen and women networked amongst themselves. Mariana surveyed the room, nervously looking around for Bartlett's blond hair, but he had not yet arrived. The attendees, with their precise haircuts and photogenic faces, milled around looking for opportunities for conversation.

There were two long banquet tables that traversed the room on the far side. Each chair had a name card placed in front of it, reserving it for the venerable veteran attendees. Round tables were spread elsewhere around the hall. Those that had arrived early enough were seated around the fresh floral centerpieces, a purple petaled arrangement that complimented the light blue tablecloths.

Mariana meandered over to the side of the room away from the bustling crowd. She stood in the corner eyeing the banquet buffet table that stretched from the entrance to the stage, and the multitude of appetizers spread out upon it. A waiter passed by, placing another platter on the table. "How much are these?" asked Mariana.

"What is she doing?" Sara harshly whispered to Barbara.

Mariana filled her tiny plate with crackers, exotic cheeses, miniature turkey sandwiches, and chocolate covered cookies. Mariana faintly heard a tapping sound that seemed full of urgency. As she looked in the general direction of the noise she saw Sara peering through the window with her hand against the glass. Mariana calmly walked over while carefully balancing her plate full of appetizers.

"Relax and hobnob with the people," said Sara, "Bartlett will be here soon. And you can put down the food." "Alright," said Mariana, annoyed, "I'll just put it in a to-go box."

"There he is," said Sara.

Mariana spotted him immediately on the other side of the room. He looked just like his picture in the real estate booklet. She returned to the chatty convention attendees. She observed them observing each other, sized them up as they sized each other up and put herself into their self-centered minds. Mariana held her cell phone to her ear as she slowly walked around soaking up information, "Ok, sure, right, I have got that, I see." She slowly crossed the room moving through the sociable gathering, catching glimpses of the attendees' hidden lives. Making her way past a sea of personalities, a conniver, an adulterer, a thief, a manipulator, and every so often a decent individual, she brushed past them all as she made her way towards Bartlett.

An older salesman in a pin-striped suit with grey flecks along the sides of his hair was deep in conversation with a shorter blonde real estate agent who looked up at him, entranced by his delivery. From the snippet of conversation she picked up, Mariana ascertained the complete nature of the discussion. He was trying to convince her to buy one of his properties under the ruse that he was strapped for cash and liquidating assets. Mariana momentarily lowered the phone and intervened, "Oh, I hope you don't mind, I just was on the phone with the original owner, it's a bad deal."
"What do you mean?" asked the woman plaintively. Mariana looked into the man's eyes, and said, "The land is worthless. It's not a new problem, it was there when you bought it, but you didn't know about it. What was it, a sinkhole? No, radiation inside the ground, so anyone that lives there will eventually start glowing." Mariana then turned to the woman, "Someone sold it to him and then he was going to sell it to you, and then you were going to sell it to that gentleman over there," Mariana pointed to a grey-haired man in a tuxedo across the room. That land is cursed, it makes a liar out of everyone that owns it, so if I were you I would stay away." The man stood aghast, ashamed, and angry. Mariana held up her cell phone, "I have to take this. Hello? Yes, of course," and went on her way, drinking in every word she heard. The business woman impolitely left the man where he was, fuming.

A defensive wall of sycophants protected Bartlett from Mariana's approach as he moved around the room. A petite woman with black hair and a short blue dress approached him, "I'm so sorry about your fiancé's passing," she said. "That's very kind of you to say," he responded. Mariana was standing several tables away behind them, and could only observe their vague body language, which spoke volumes.

"Where is he?" asked Barbara, "Does she have him?"

"I think he's over there," said Sara. At that moment Bartlett stepped in front of the window and turned to look outside. They both simultaneously ducked below the window.

"Did he see us?" asked Barbara.

"No," Sara whispered, "because he's not looking for us, because he doesn't suspect a thing. We're going to get you, Bartlett."

"He's got clean nostrils," remarked Barbara as she looked upwards.

Bartlett ran his fingers across his hair and turned to rejoin the crowd.

Bartlett walked away, Mariana trailing behind him.

As Mariana passed by, Sara frantically tapped on the window again. Mariana stopped and reluctantly took a couple of steps backwards. She leaned over, almost pressing her head against the window. "I've got you and about two-hundred spirits all telling me what to do at the same time. What is it, child?"

"The security guards are watching you." Mariana made eye contact with one of them and said to Sara, "I don't have much time. I'm not done yet. The spirits are talking so fast I can barely understand them. I have never seen spirits like these. I have to get close to him."

"You don't need to," pleaded Sara, "just look at him and figure it out."

"I have to touch him," said Mariana persistently.

The security guards left their post and began to move towards Mariana.

"Alright, go," whispered Sara.

The fraudulent businessman that had been exposed by Mariana was standing behind the guards with a smirk on his face. Mariana eyed Bartlett's blond hair and began to move towards him. The guards wound around tables, closing in. She pushed her way past two idle saleswomen who each squealed in turn. The commotion was arousing the attention of the other real estate agents.

Bartlett was surrounded by a throng of attendees. Though they were densely packed, Mariana found a brief opening and was able to slide through. She accidentally knocked over a woman's plate of cheeses as she squeezed by. "Pardon me." She was still several layers back from Bartlett as she glanced back to see the guards also entering the crowd. She looked around and noted that there were two old acquaintances standing next to each other, but neither had broken the ice. Mariana surreptitiously tapped one of the women on the shoulder, causing her to look over at the old friend and greet her with a handshake, which blocked one of the guards as he tried to reach Mariana. She pushed past two more attendees, and attained eye contact with Bartlett as he took notice of the commotion approaching him. Mariana pushed closer until she was directly in front of him. "What is she doing?!" said Sara.

She stretched out her arm towards him just as both of the security guards seized her. Her fingertips were stopped just inches from his face, and he drew back, startled.

Mariana struggled to break free as the guards dragged her away, the commotion stirring the crowd. Mind reading aside, Sara was impressed by Mariana's own spirit, she was definitely trying to earn Barbara's money. Judging by the way she fought against the guards it looked like she hadn't gotten what she came for. Barbara nudged Sara and asked, "Do you want to go?" "No," replied Sara, having decided that she would ascertain as much as she could about Bartlett now that Mariana was out of the picture.

A middle-aged woman with a sharp black business suit and a mechanical make-up application technique walked past the long banquet table and stopped behind a podium, tapping on the microphone to make sure it was on, "Excuse me," she said, leaning over the podium, "Excuse me." The murmurs of the socializing crowd subsided as she continued, "We have a very courageous speaker with us today. He has endured a heart-breaking tragedy recently, but he insisted that he be here. Everybody please welcome Adam Bartlett."

The convention hall was filled with polite applause. Sara's hand clenched into a tight fist. He was capitalizing on her death, using her to aggrandize himself. She felt that she didn't even need Mariana here at this point, it didn't matter, she could have come alone, she had seen enough. The tightening in her stomach grew as the throng applauded Bartlett.

As he stood at the podium he scanned around the room looking for Mariana, but she was no longer there. Seeing that all was clear, he began to speak, "You may not have known her, but my fiancé Joy was my inspiration. She was my muse. Though our time together was brief, I will always have her to cherish and inspire me. That's why I wanted to speak to you today about the importance of finding a passion to focus your mind and drive you in your work."
Sara found it difficult to read behind his words.

Behind Bartlett the white tablecloth hanging over the edge of the banquet table began to rustle. Then Mariana suddenly emerged from underneath the table and quickly got to her feet after having crawled the length of the entire room under the table on her hands and knees, being careful to avoid being detected as she crawled through the shifting gauntlet of diners' legs.

66

He didn't even notice her out of the corner of his eye until it was too late.

Mariana grabbed hold of his wrist with one hand, and with the other she pressed her fingers against his palm. Bartlett was in shock and tried to pull away. She quickly and forcefully ran her fingers across the lines on his palm while she stared straight into his eyes.

CHAPTER 14

Driving back from the jail, Barbara felt like she was settling into a routine, having bailed out a prisoner yet again. Mariana sat in the backseat quietly murmuring to the supposed spirits around her. Sara was in Barbara's house watching a succession of soap operas. After she saw them drive up she ran to the door to greet them as they walked in, "How much was it this time?" "They're raising their prices," said Barbara as she and Mariana entered the house and headed for the kitchen. There were already two cups of coffee waiting for them, just as Barbara had politely suggested.

All three of them sat around the kitchen table. Sara watched Barbara and Mariana take their first sips of coffee, and said in a low tone of voice, "Tell me."
"A dark spirit…" said Mariana.
"What about Joy?"
"No joy in his heart…"
Impatient, Sara interrupted her, "What about his fiancé?"
Mariana replied patiently, "No Joy in his heart." She looked off in the distance as if she was distracted, focusing on

something important, then she added, "He loved her. I can see it." Sara was incredulous hearing this complete reversal, but Mariana closed her eyes again and screwed her face into an expression of painful concentration, then opened her eyes again, "He loved her like…she was, I can see it…an object, not a spirit…an ornament. He loved her for the way she made him look. He loved himself. That's what he loved. He bought her diamonds…only because she was his…jewelry." Sara was decidedly impressed by Mariana's insight. With only a few moments with Bartlett she was able to discern the dynamic of his relationship with Joy, and the underpinnings of his crime. His superficiality degraded Joy into being an object. There must have come a time when he no longer considered her to be a worthy belonging, and so he discarded her.

Then Mariana continued, "He thought she was a spoiled brat. Sour like milk. Pretty outside and sour on the inside."

"Joy wasn't like that," said Sara, recoiling, "You've read it wrong."

"She's just reading it through his eyes," said Barbara.

"He didn't respect her enough to risk prison for her," said Mariana.

Suddenly Mariana's reading had taken a turn, and it defied Sara's long held assessment. "How could you know that?" Sara asked.

"Because I looked through his eyes and measured his soul. He is not the killer."

CHAPTER 15

She was filled with rage, then shame, then desperation. Emotions swung through her mind, pulling her in several directions at once. She didn't want to believe it. Could she really have been accusing an innocent man? She was conflicted and confused, unsure what to feel about Bartlett, and what to feel about the murderer, now that they were two separate people. The hatred she had felt for Bartlett was replaced by fear of the murderer. The killer was not only out there, but no one was looking for her. If it wasn't a crime of passion then it could happen again.

Defiance took root in Sara's mind as it often did in times of extreme stress. Sara still had faith in her own intuition despite Mariana's conviction that Bartlett was innocent. Maybe Bartlett wasn't the killer, but he had to have been involved in some way. He probably had someone else do it for him. He wasn't the killer like Mariana said, but he was still Joy's murderer.

"You know, Barbara," said Sara as she looked at herself in the mirror and brushed her hair to the side with her fingers, "I'm not trying to run away at this moment, it's just that I promised Brad that I would see him."

"Is she really telling the truth, Mariana?" asked Barbara.

"She is," came the reply.

"It really is handy having you around."

After dropping by her apartment, Sara drove towards Brad's beach house and resolved to put the whole situation out of her mind, temporarily at least. She didn't want to be on edge during her crucial second date with Brad. Working with Mariana had opened her eyes to how subtle communication can be. A passing thought can pass across the face and speak volumes. A minor expression can lay everything bare. She carried her purse on her shoulder and in her hand carried a pitcher of cold margaritas, a gift to take Brad's mind off his predicament.

"Hey, you're running late." He was lounging in a homemade adirondack chair on the deck, either resting or working on a tan. He wore white shorts and a cute yellow t-shirt. The sunlight reflected brightly off the ocean, and illuminated the white beach.

"What's that?" he asked with a smile, gesturing to the green pitcher in Sara's hand.

"Secret weapon," she replied.

"Good timing. The fish is just about done." He picked up a dinner plate off the deck railing and then walked over to the grill standing on the deck, thin wisps of smoke rose from it and disappeared in the breeze. He opened the lid and revealed two beautiful sizzling fish being grilled on tin-foil. The aroma of the sizzling juices were enough to rouse Sara's appetite. He poked some long metal tongs into the grill and lifted each grilled fish onto the plate.

He followed Sara down the walkway, her dress swaying as she sashayed, bouncing against her thighs. In-between the end of the walkway and the edge of the tide stood a wooden picnic table. The boards had the battered look about them that meant Brad had salvaged them from the ocean.

Sara gazed out at the lengthy shoreline. The beach had been picked clean of wreckage for the day. The only sign of debris was a small two-man sailboat that was stranded on the shore like a beached whale. It was halfway buried in the sand, its mast was tilted at a thirty degree angle and the sails were hanging loose and flapping gently with the breeze.

Brad tenderly set out fish on each of their plates.

"I think you are going to like this," said Sara. Two tall glasses had been sat on top of napkins so that they wouldn't blow away.

They each took a seat at the table. She poured the pitcher of half-frozen margaritas into each glass. The sweet green liquid oozed into each glass. Brad lifted his glass to his lips and took a sip.

"This is the best margarita I've ever had."

"Barbara and I rescued an old cocinero in Mexico and he gave her the recipe. I'll write it down for you. She pulled out a notepad and pen from her purse and scribbled down,

Barbara's Margaritas:
Equal parts:
Triple-sec
Tequila
Margarita mixer
1/3 part orange juice
Fill it up with ice and blend it, you're set.

"What do you mean one-third part orange juice?" asked Brad.
"Say you had one cup each of tequila and the other stuff you

would add one-third cup orange juice."

"Oh."

Sara speared a fish with her fork, the hot meat almost slid off the bone.

"This table that we're eating on," said Brad, "it used to be the roof over someone's head. Do you like it? I feel like, what was his name...Nero, playing his fiddle while Rome burns down. Have you ever been around here during a storm?"

"No."

"The next time the wind picks up, and the ocean tide swells, and the thunder starts shaking the island, I want you right here with me. You've never seen anything like it."

The fish tasted like it had been caught minutes earlier. Brad had added just the right amount of pepper to it. Sara could tell that Brad was proud of himself as she ate his fish and sat at his table.

"Have you found a house yet?" asked Brad.

"What do you mean?"

"You were shopping for a house last time."

Sara suddenly remembered her fabrication, "Oh, I haven't found one yet."

She delicately picked apart the fish before her. It was crispy in the right places and tender in the others. The sweet char complemented the succulent meat. She washed it down with her fresh margarita which provided a mild soothing sting as it slid down her throat and a kick of warmth that eased into her mind.

"Living on the edge out here has taught me to appreciate everything around me," said Brad, "It makes me realize how much I don't want to give it up. It would be nice if this place was a houseboat, and when the ocean surged up we could just sit on the porch and drink margaritas, and watch it come in, and then the house would just lift up and float along on the waves until the ocean quieted back down."

"These past few weeks I've been spending a lot of time at the beach," said Sara, "I don't even know why, really. It just pulls me in the more time I spend here. I just melt in the sunshine. It's hard to describe. And it's so nice not having to wear shoes. I wish there were sidewalks made out of sand."

"It's because you have such pretty toes, you want to show them off. I've always felt like the beach was magical. It's the only place where it's socially acceptable for a woman to walk around in her underwear. No, there's a lot more to it than that. You know, back in the seventeen-hundreds, back before doctors had any modern medicine, if someone was sick they would write out a prescription telling them to go to the ocean. They said the salt air would invigorate the blood and cure their maladies. I think they were on to something. We're more alive at the beach. It's a scientific fact. There's more oxygen in the air at sea level. Those businessmen working in skyscrapers, they're suffocating up there. You shouldn't feel bad about it. There is nothing like being here. It's paradise. Paradise isn't a state of mind, it's a place. Nobody goes looking for paradise in a garbage heap. They come to the beach."

"That's a shallow definition of paradise. I think you are the first person I've met that would admit to being shallow. And you're proud of it too?"

"There's nothing wrong with being shallow," said Brad, "Anyone who thinks there is is not living in reality. Why do people go to the beach? They go because the beach is pretty to look at. When you're able to look at something beautiful every day it has an effect on who you are. It makes you think pretty thoughts and feel pretty emotions. We're shallow creatures by nature. Beauty has a profound effect upon us. That's why we have super models, million dollar paintings, shiny cars, tropical screen-savers…"

"Beauty is the deepest thing of all," echoed Sara. "You

remind me of a friend I had. She was one of the beautiful things in life. Some people only liked her because she was beautiful."

"God, I try so hard to memorize it," said Brad, "I stare out at the beach and the waves and the horizon stretching out to infinity, and I try to fix it in my mind like a photograph so that I can always be here, no matter what happens to me, but it's too complex, my brain can't hold it all at once, only pieces. Sometimes I feel like I can come back here in these short vivid bursts, but the beach doesn't stay fixed in my mind for long, it slips away, the tide that goes out and does not come back. A place like this, you can only come here in dreams. I don't know why, but that's the only way to capture it and immerse yourself in it."

"That's why you're working so hard to save this place."

"Not working, fighting. This latest skirmish in this long battle. I have to fend it off until the tide retreats, and then I can reclaim my beach and declare victory. What are you smirking at? This is a war. A hammer for a gun and nails for ammunition. I feel like I'm stronger than nature, so if I can make this house as strong as me then the ocean won't stand a chance. Maybe we're not supposed to live so close to something so beautiful." He brushed a lock of hair away from her eyes, "What do you think?"

Sara felt calm around him because he seemed to know where he was going. The confusion that she had been experiencing was washed away for the moment by his certitude. He was facing an obstacle just as profound, but he knew exactly how to fight it, and he knew that he had what he needed in order to win. She wondered if her fragile state of mind was making her fall for his strength. No, it wasn't that. There was something else about him. The way he clung to beauty so fiercely, like an artist. She understood that when he looked at her he was telling her that she was beautiful.

"Having something pretty to look at is a worthy goal in life," he said as he gazed into her eyes, "It could be the key to everything. The things you stare at deeply, they become a part of you."

He took her by the hand as they walked along the walkway towards the house. As he carried her into his bedroom she couldn't decide which she enjoyed more, his philosophical defense of shallowness, or his muscles.

CHAPTER 16

When Sara awoke the next morning she spent the first few moments of her day staring at Brad's thick eyelashes and rounded shoulders. She wondered if she was rushing the relationship. No, she knew she was rushing the relationship, and she could only imagine what Barbara would say about it. She knew she was being reckless, but she didn't care. Maybe after all that had happened she needed someone like Brad to make her feel secure. He was up against an enemy and wasn't deterred. She was grateful to have this time with Brad as a respite from her troubles.

Brad was wrapped in his bedsheet, sleeping soundly until Sara's cell phone loudly rang. Sara reached over and fumbled through her purse, then held the phone to her ear.
"Hello?" There was silence on the other end. Then a commanding voice spoke up, "Sara, this is detective Cole. I need to see you."

She headed straight to Barbara's house.
"All he said is that there is a grand jury, and he wants to see

me at the beach this afternoon," said Sara to Barbara. They were standing in Barbara's foyer, Sara had just taken off her shoes. "A grand jury. That's interesting," replied Barbara. Sara then heard a sound coming from Barbara's pristine living room.

She looked in and saw Mariana there, sleeping soundly on the couch. She was scantily dressed, wearing only her purple bra and panties on her lean body, and golden rings on her fingers. She was snuggled up with an exotic looking voodoo doll tucked under her arm. It had wild hair and a zig-zag mouth but Mariana cradled it as if it were a baby. Sara stood over her, disapprovingly. "New houseguest?" "Hrumpt, destiny, arwph," mumbled Mariana quietly to herself.

Sara was going to say more but didn't want to upset Barbara because she wanted her to be in an open state of mind. That was always necessary for getting Barbara to do something that she didn't want to do.

"It's ok," said Barbara with her full voice, "she's out like a light."

"That detective won't tell me the entire story," continued Sara, "I want to know everything that is going on, so we're going to need someone on the inside."

"Oh, lord," said Barbara, "I hope you're not talking about who I think you're talking about."

"You can handle it just one more time," pleaded Sara.

"I've got my eye on some other men at the moment."

"Oh, come on."

"Not for a million summers."

"Please?"

"No."

"No?"

"No."

Sara clasped her hands beneath her chin and leaned close to Barbara, "Please, please, pretty please." Sara had a self-satisfied smile.

Barbara sighed, "It's only a favor if you really appreciate it."

"I will."

"Because otherwise, it's just another awful date with that man."

CHAPTER 17

The walls of the interior were solid stone bricks stacked to the ceiling and framed with stout aged wooden beams. The only lighting came from dim low-hanging lamps that hovered over each table. When Barbara arrived at the restaurant the Judge was waiting for her, and had been for twenty minutes. She was wearing her light blue number with the matching purple heels, the Judge's favorite. She was looking forward to meeting the Judge about as much as a convict who was waiting to be sentenced.

He was standing regally in the waiting area. Despite his frown-framing jowls, wrinkled brow, dark grey barbershop hair, and an out of fashion snug fitting black suit, he actually looked handsome. He was a well-fed bachelor, his heft showed it. He ate at pricey restaurants regardless of whether he had a date or not. He looked at her with his good-natured light blue eyes. "Every time I see you, you look better and better. You're aging like French wine," he said, "You look better than you did twenty years ago."

"Ugly people age well because they have no beauty to lose,"

said Barbara.

"Come now," he admonished, "you're out of order."

The breeze blew the detective's hair across the opposite direction he had combed it, so he constantly ran his fingers through his hair, wanting to both look professional, and keep facing away from the ocean as he stood expecting the arrival of Sara. She eventually appeared from behind the dunes wearing a tight grey t-shirt, khaki shorts, and tennis shoes. Detective Cole stood stone still as a child ran around him to catch a Frisbee. His eyes narrowed on his narrow face as Sara approached him. He was wrapped in a black coat that concealed any weapons he might be wearing. He was still dressed in his formal clothes, his nice shoes half-buried in the sand. He was one of those rare individuals that lived and worked right by the beach, and yet never spent much time there.

A waitress led Barbara and the Judge to an isolated booth in the corner, the Judge had no doubt told her to bring them there for the sake of privacy. The Judge was an embarrassingly messy eater.

The only time Barbara ever came to this restaurant was when she was accompanied by the Judge. She and Sara never went to this place, the atmosphere was stiff and the lighting was awkward, it was not unlike a courtroom. As soon as they took their seats another waitress walked over carrying two large plates of food. "I went ahead and ordered for the both of us," said the Judge, "I hope you don't mind. Crab legs, your favorite." The waitress sat a plate before each of them and yet another waitress arrived with a bottle of white wine, pouring each of them a full glass before setting the bottle down and politely leaving. Despite herself, Barbara was flattered at receiving her favorite meal, and allowed herself to smile.

"You lose ten years when you smile," he said.

"Have you read the paper today?" the detective asked Sara.
"No, is there some actual news in it?" she asked in return.
"It keeps getting worse and worse out there," he replied with an edge in his voice.
Sara began walking down the beach and the detective followed her lead.
"I guess you finally gave up on the pawn shop angle?"
"No, we just haven't found the old guy yet, but we're working on it."
Sara shook her head.
"But you might be interested to know," he continued, "that it was Joy's ring that he sold, and that tomorrow I am going to personally return it to Bartlett. While he's in the station I'm going to go ahead and ask him a few questions."

The Judge picked up the crab mallet that the waitress had left beside the platter and he set it off to the side, then reached into his coat pocket and pulled out his own small oak hammer, his courtroom gavel. He carefully positioned his dinner knife over a crab's claw, then he slammed the gavel down upon it with all the authority of adjourning a contentious, high-stakes murder trial, and the claw cracked open revealing the fresh meat inside.
"Do you appreciate my table manners?" he asked. "I took notes during our last date. When you say things I listen to them and I take them to heart. I know you want to see me become a better man."
"Are you talking about the time I called you a grizzly bear after you attacked that plate of salmon?" she asked.
"I've been taking smaller bites. Speaking of biting off more than you can chew, I was wondering what you were doing bailing out that fortune teller?"

"Oh, that was nothing," Barbara said, "You know, sometimes friendships look like entanglements from the outside."

"Strange company," he remarked, "I think it is very noble of you, the way you take in runaways."

"We've got a pretty strong lead," said the detective, "you got your wish, Sara. We're officially calling in Bartlett for questioning."

"That's terrific," stammered Sara, "What evidence have you got on him?"

"Not a thing," he replied, "I thought I would try to size him up and see if I can find any inconsistencies, the normal routine. I thought you might have some questions you would want me to ask him. Since you knew her."

They were not far from where Joy's body had been found. The beach had completely returned to normal, as if it had never happened. Sara guessed that those crime scene body outlines didn't last long in the sand.

"You want to find out everything he knows," said Sara, "if you can piece together their relationship I think you will find out why he did it. He may have even been cheating on her."

"I've been keeping an eye on him. I think that, you have probably picked up on it too, that everything he has ever desired or achieved has had to do with women. His quality of life, his appearance, his possessions, they aren't the real goals in his life, they are just the means to an end. I'll bet that he's the sort of guy that when he looks into the mirror he's not really able to figure out who exactly he is looking at. The only mirror he looks into is the eyes of a woman."

The Judge was captivated by Barbara's eyes. "It's a strange case, alright, which means it's a bad time to be in strange company. They're putting together a grand jury already."

"Oh, really," Barbara said, feigning disinterest, "they must have some good evidence then."

"Evidence? A lack of evidence doesn't slow anyone down these days. You know how it goes. Someone doesn't do their job and so it makes mine that much harder. They don't have to deal with it, they just move on to something else."

"That's a shame, Judge. Then they don't know anything at all?"

"No," he said as he put more crab meat in his mouth, "these detectives think like juries. All they know is story-telling. The guilty party is the one whose story doesn't make sense, and Sara Steinberg's is over the moon."

Barbara raised an eyebrow, "Oh? So they're after Sara?"

CHAPTER 18

"He will probably act innocent," said Sara, "but don't buy it. He's a salesman. Just get close to him and if you let him talk enough he will convict himself."
The detective listened with interest.

As the Judge tried to soothe her with pleasantries, Barbara rooted around in her purse until she found her cell phone. "Don't bother wearing perfume next time," he said, "I'll bring you a dozen roses." The Judge abruptly stopped speaking as Barbara pulled out her phone and clicked the speed-dial for Sara.

The phone rang loudly in Sara's purse. She glanced at the number before she clicked the phone off. Barbara's complaints about the Judge would have to wait. "I told Joy to leave him from the beginning," she continued, "She wouldn't listen."

Barbara and the Judge stared silently at each other across the table until Sara's voice-mail finally picked up, "Honey, give me a call when you get this, thanks." She put the phone back into her purse.

Barbara didn't even have to look at him. She knew he was riled up because he was paying far more attention to her than he was to his food. She glanced over. Sure enough, his cheeks had reddened, and it wasn't from the marinara.

"I'll call you tomorrow for another meeting and let you know how it goes," said the detective, "Thanks for your cooperation, Sara. I won't be able to do this without you."
"Anytime," she replied, feeling a combination of gratitude and anticipation.

Sara called out to him as he went, "Make sure you can get a conviction." He turned back briefly to face her, "I intend to," and then turned back and walked down the windy boardwalk.

The Judge had one eyebrow cocked and a scowl across his face. Apparently he had put it all together. 'He must be getting wiser with age,' thought Barbara.
"You just came here on an errand then?" he asked, "No, it wasn't an errand like shopping, it was a chore, wasn't it, like taking out the trash."

If there hadn't been some truth to it she wouldn't have been struck so forcefully by his words, she preferred him when he was irrational. "With all the things you have put me through Judge, you do not have the right to be melodramatic right now."
"You know I didn't come here to bring up our history," he said plaintively, "I only wanted to ask you a question."
She was intrigued by his change of tone, it wasn't like him to back down from a fit of anger. He seemed unusually apprehensive, as if his outburst was only a symptom of his

nerves. He clasped his hands and looked at her with intensity and trepidation.

"What do you think about marriage?"

'Well, he definitely isn't getting wiser,' thought Barbara. "A life sentence," she said.

"Sometimes," he replied, "a life sentence isn't so bad."

"Compared to a death sentence."

"It depends on how you do your time. Do you really think that I would make you live in a prison?"

"I didn't say that. I said you would be the prison."

"It's only a prison if you want to leave."

"I must be guilty of something to wind up here," replied Barbara as she glanced at the exit.

"Don't you feel guilty?"

"Of what, contempt?"

"I was going to say fraud," he shot back, "Or vandalism, breaking my heart the way you do."

"Do you object?" asked Barbara.

"I do."

"On what grounds?"

"Misleading the witness," he said indignantly.

Barbara stood up and slung the strap of her purse across her shoulder.

"Don't come around asking for any more favors from me," spat the Judge.

Barbara's hips swung from side to side as she strutted out of the restaurant in her high heels.

"Fine. Fleeing the scene of an accident. That's always Barbara!"

Filled with a frustration that only Barbara could bring him, the Judge slammed his gavel against the table, sending shards of crab shell flying.

CHAPTER 19

Normally around this time of day she would be sitting
leisurely outside a coffee shop, a warm cup in her hand and
enough stolen glances from passersby to keep her amused.
Instead, Sara walked beside the busy stores of the promenade
mulling things over, and coped with the gnawing hunger in her
stomach. She had completely forgotten to eat. She wondered
if the detective would actually be able to handle Bartlett. If it
wasn't done right then Bartlett could slip right through their
fingers. He had seemed to fool Mariana, and she was a
pseudo-professional, the police department may not fare much
better. Lilly's Hot Dog Stand suddenly woke her from her
reverie. The aroma of the hot beef franks drifted on the
breeze. There was only a short line in front of the yellow and
red striped hot dog cart. Sara stood at the back of the line
behind the cart. Around the promenade the shops were doing
brisk business. Young shirtless men swaggered in and out of
the surf shop in pairs. Young ladies drifted in and out of the
craft shops looking over the latest in décor, and women
walked along with full shopping bags, some from the Beauty

Queen Dress Shop no doubt. They all seemed in jovial spirits as they went about their day.

"Next." The entire rainbow of bikinis had coasted through and it was Sara's turn. "I'll take a big one with some mustard." The older woman working at the stand generously slathered some mustard on the hot dog and looked at Sara the whole time with a quizzical expression on her face.

"Do I know you?"

Sara looked at the woman again, her grayish blond hair, rounded bulb of a nose, droopy chin, and over-sized bosom. She thought to herself that the woman could have been recalling any number of times or places, and she was hoping that it wasn't most of those times or places. But she would recognize this woman if she had seen her at any time before, and her face didn't ring a bell. Still, the woman persisted, "I've seen you somewhere. Do you know my granddaughter? She sells bras at the lingerie store."

"I've probably met her," said Sara, though she couldn't remember exactly when.

"Oh, well. I'll think of it eventually."

"Alright," said Sara, easing out of the conversation, "nice meeting you." "Again," added the woman.

Sara walked along to the open area with park benches and stood in the shade with other diners. Standing next to her, a red-haired lightly freckled girl in a light yellow bikini was munching on a beef frank. She was also checking out the passing shoppers until her gaze drifted over to Sara, and then she stopped chewing. Sara noticed out of the corner of her eye that the girl was staring at her. Sara glanced over and met her eyes. The girl's eyes then bulged and panic fell over her face as she grasped her throat and began to silently cough. Sara dropped her own hot dog to the ground and firmly hit the girl on the back with her open palm. The red haired girl then loudly hacked a cough, hurriedly chewed her food, glanced over at Sara, and walked away, murmuring, "Thanks" as she went.

Sara noticed a distinguished older woman sitting on a bench as the people passed her by on the sidewalk. Her long light green dress complemented the dark green shade of the bench. This was certainly not an accident. She was sitting on the same green bench that she sat on day after day and week after week. It was a good way to people-watch without having to wear a bathing suit. She carried bags under her eyes which drooped down towards her upturned nose, held eruditely in the air. She wore an old-fashioned pale yellow hat that would look fashionable on a younger head. She had the appearance of a widow whose grandkids didn't visit often enough. She sat slowly turning over the pages, perusing the newspaper in this way, like she always did, when Sara noticed a picture of Joy on the front page.

"Excuse me, are you done with this paper?"

"Of course I'm not done with it," she said.

"Sorry, I just meant the front page," Sara explained.

The woman lifted the newspaper back up and continued reading. The bottom half of the paper was still resting on her lap. Sara leaned down and craned her neck around to try and make out the text below Joy's picture.

"Could you lift it a little higher?" asked Sara. The woman began to protest, "Why don't you..." but then stopped. She looked down at the paper in her hand and then back up at Sara. She then handed it over and eyed Sara curiously.

Sara held up the newspaper and it may as well have been a mirror because her own picture was staring back at her. It was her old mugshot from the time she was caught breaking into that doll factory. She had a defiant look on her face that somewhat admitted her guilt. They could have at least used a more recent one when her hair was in order.

Sara was bemused. The newspaper editor, Celestine,

was still upset with Sara about that episode a few years ago when Sara had accidentally locked her and the church choir nuns in the church basement and, until Sunday morning, they had to live off of canned food that was intended for the homeless. 'Celestine still can't carry a tune,' Sara thought, 'but she sure can hold a grudge.'

The article cited Bartlett as being Joy's fiancé, though they didn't bother to look into their relationship at all. At least Bartlett was mentioned in the story, it was better than nothing. Sara continued reading: "Locals are worried. A concerned citizen at Morton Pastries commented between bites of banana pudding, 'Sara [Steinberg] was close to her. Right up to the end. There is something not right about the case. Sara was talking to her. Someone was pretending to be Joy, honey. There's an impostor out there.' "

"Honey? Banana pudding !? That's Barbara!" Sara was flabbergasted, and spoke out loud despite herself.

Sara scanned down to the end of the article which mentioned more about the mood of the town, and she caught a glimpse of her name. She was noted as a 'person of interest.'

Sara remembered that the detective had asked if she had read the newspaper. At least he was doing something about it, interviewing Bartlett to set the record straight. In the meantime though, she would be a suspect in the public eye, and there was nothing she could do about it.

'At least they put Bartlett in the story too,' she reminded herself.

"Can I keep this?" Sara asked the older woman sweetly.

"You might as well," the woman huffed.

The street seemed unusually full of people. They were brushing past each other at a fast clip, trying to avoid bogging down in congestion. The mood amongst them seemed off, tense. The sunny sky and balmy winds suggested brighter attitudes than the ones possessed of the passersby. They were on edge, alert. Sara could feel the glances that bounced off her from all directions, from across the street, a driver casually looking in her direction as he drove by. Two women were window shopping, already carrying full shopping bags at their sides. One of them made eye contact with Sara, then looked away. As Sara shuddered and turned her back the woman was thinking to herself that she would like to have a shirt like the one Sara was wearing, where did she buy it?

Sara turned her face towards the reflective glass window of a local crafts shop. Her face was reflected back, darkened circles of sleeplessness and all, with all the watchful pedestrians behind her moving by. Some of them seemed to be making eye contact with her reflection. Behind the glass window, inside the small shop, someone who had been perusing a shelf of decorative candles was now watching Sara's every move, looking into her eyes as Sara looked into her own.

Suzanne put down the cherry-scented candles she was going to buy and left through the side door.

CHAPTER 20

Back at her apartment, Sara sorted through her stack of mail. One letter had Sara's name handwritten in calligraphy like a formal wedding invitation. She opened it and read the ornately written but simply stated message inside, "You are invited to appear at Suzanne Stripling's home this Friday night."

Sara tossed the invitation aside. She had no intention of wasting her time at the party, and she didn't want to give Suzanne the satisfaction of having reeled her in. 'If Barbara's so interested she can go herself,' Sara thought.

Sara remembered that she had a date with Brad that night. She didn't know how she would explain her appearance in the newspaper. More importantly, she didn't know how she would keep it a secret from him to begin with. They were just beginning their relationship and already the secrets she had held were catching up with her. She wondered if he would be understanding in spite of her behavior. She knew she would have to break it to him eventually. Regardless, on her way to Barbara's she stopped by Brad's driveway and picked up his newspaper.

Sara was holding the newspaper in front of Barbara at the kitchen table.

"What?" said Barbara, "That no-good hussy! I was just having a conversation with her, I didn't think she would...I guess you must have ticked her off at some point."

"That thing with the nuns."

"Oh, right."

The kitchen phone then began to ring loudly. Sara reached over for the phone. "Don't answer it!" Barbara shouted. Sara startled back. "Mariana, will you get that for me?" Barbara called out.

Mariana was comfortably nestled in Barbara's luxurious couch surrounded by piles of decorative pillows, and was watching her favorite daytime talk show. She couldn't bear to watch daytime soap operas, or any scripted show for that matter. She could never completely buy into them because she was never fooled like everyone else. No matter who the actor was, she could always tell they were pretending, and so even Emmy winning performances rang hollow.

Mariana clicked the mute button on the remote to silence the arguing estranged lovers, then got up and casually walked into the kitchen, allowing the phone to ring three times before she was able to answer it. When she picked up the phone she spoke in her most polite, secretarial voice, "Barbara's residence, who's speaking?" Barbara watched as Mariana listened to the caller. Mariana nodded and then handed the phone to Barbara. "It's clean," she whispered, and she walked back into the living room.

After Barbara held the phone to her ear her expression went blank, and she fell silent. Sara held her breath for a moment. Then Barbara's disposition returned to normal. "It's just the Judge," she said as she hung up the phone and sat back down at the table.

Sara held her head in her clammy hands. "What am I going to do? They're making it look like I'm the impostor." Barbara put her hand on Sara's shoulder. "Just calm down, honey. I know that you're innocent. Mariana knows that you're innocent, of this at least. That's all that matters right now."

"You're right," said Sara, the tension in her voice easing off.

Barbara had a way of saying the right things to calm her down, she had a lot of practice at it. Whenever a situation seemed impossible to escape, Barbara could always show her the way out. Sara was pacified, taking refuge in her friendship once again. She felt lighter, free from the worrying that had plagued her.

"So," said Sara, "how did it go with the Judge?"

"They're trying to convict you," Barbara replied.

CHAPTER 21

There was a gentle ambiance around Wiley's Oyster Bar and Grill. Overlooking the serene evening ocean and the night sky, the framing of the decking was built around tall wind-carved oak trees that were contorted into twisted architecture. A soft glow emanated from strings of white Christmas tree lights wrapped around the boughs of the trees, swaying gently with the salty breeze. They populated the sky overhead with the light of a thousand constellations. Little multi-colored paper umbrellas shaded martinis from the Christmas tree lights above. A young girl in a light pink dress and sandals was rhythmically moving from side to side and shaking a maraca in her hand with the beat. At second glance, Sara thought the maraca looked exactly like her sand-filled cell phone.

Sara, Brad, and Barbara sat around a round rustic wooden table which had been fashioned from the planks of a shrimp boat. Their faces were warmly lit, and they had the air of aristocrats, all of them being formally dressed. Sara was sitting pretty in her black dress and diamond earrings. Her hair was done up with pins. Barbara's red dress and necklace of pearls complimented her red heels nicely, and Brad was wearing a dashing black suit and tie. His brown hair was combed to one side, and he wore some short stubble on his face. Barbara couldn't help herself, she reached over and pinched his cheek, "Isn't he cute?" He smiled broadly and locked eyes with Sara.

Without even taking their order, a waiter walked over to their table and laid down a plate stacked with the tall legs of a king crab. Right behind him a waitress arrived and sat an empty glass in front of Sara and Barbara, and then filled the glasses to the brim with white wine.

"We've got an understanding with the owner," said Sara, "don't we?" "Oh yeah," said Barbara.

Sara took a sip of her wine. "He owes us big time," she said, "We come here every Friday for a free meal."

"Sara told me about your prime real estate," said Barbara, "I doubt there's anything to worry about, darling. Hurricane season's over."

Sara had insisted that Barbara come along, to impress Brad with her glamour and geniality.

"Do you think Jay will mind if I grab another bottle of wine?" Sara asked. "He usually doesn't," said Barbara, knowing that the owner was a very generous man, "Go ahead." Sara got up from the table and sought out a fresh bottle.

Brad then turned to Barbara, genuinely curious about this intriguing woman, "Sara has told me all about you, but I still don't know what you do for a living."

"We just live for a living, that keeps us busy enough," said Barbara.

"But how do you earn a living?"

Barbara leaned in close, letting him know that she was about to reveal something special, "I'll tell you. It's rare, but sometimes money will rain down from the sky, and when that happens Sara and I will open up our purses and run around and scoop it up. It wasn't always like this. I spent many years working in a daycare looking after the least humble of all God's creatures. It seems like as soon as I met her things started working out for the better. She doesn't always have a good head on her shoulders, but she is nosy. She's got a good nose on her face."

"What are you two conspiring about?" asked Sara as she returned with with a full bottle of white wine.

"I was just telling him about me and you. Remember when I found you, you were living in a pyramid." Sara rolled her eyes. "It wasn't a pyramid." Barbara rolled her eyes even more dramatically, "What was that stuff written on the walls? It wasn't graffiti, it was hieroglyphs."

"I don't want to talk about my pyramid apartment."

"We don't have to, now that you've admitted that it was a pyramid."

Sara's cell phone rang, and she answered, "Hello?"

"Hello, Ms. Steinberg." She knew that voice, it was Stacey, one of the newspaper reporters. The voice continued, "Can I ask you a few questions about your relationship-" Sara shut off her phone. "Wrong number."

Jay Wiley, the owner of the restaurant, approached the table. A welcoming smile was already present on his slender face. His lanky frame drifted to the table and Sara noticed the newspaper tucked under his arm. "Hey. I hope everything is the way you like it?"

"How are you?" asked Sara.

"Fine, you? Actually, I was wondering if you would sign this newspaper, for history's sake," he said cordially. "No, no," protested Sara, but it was too late. He laid the newspaper on the table. On the front page, for everyone to see, was a picture of Barbara in handcuffs. It was the old issue from years ago. Sara breathed a sigh of relief. Jay handed Barbara a pen. "Oh, good times," said Barbara as she autographed it. Jay continued, "And Sara, if you would sign this one from today that would be perfect." He pulled out the newspaper and laid it right in front of her. Brad picked up the paper before she could say anything. There she was, her mugshot's defiant gaze staring back at him.

"What is this?" She could read the dismay on his face as he read the paper. "What in the world is going on here?" He scanned over the article.

"Brad that's a mistake. Joy was in a relationship with Bartlett."

"Real nice. You already know that I don't like Bartlett. Now you're accusing him. Have you been lying to me this whole time?"

"It was more of an omission," she replied sheepishly, "I was trying to keep things simple."

"Then maybe you should find a simple-minded boyfriend." He turned to Jay. "I hope you don't mind if I take this. Someone stole mine this morning." With that, he rose from the table and hurriedly left Sara behind.

"Brad, don't leave," she pleaded, but he was already on his feet. He was surely confused about the situation and didn't know what to think, but he did know one thing for sure, Sara had not been honest with him. He knew that she had been hiding something from him. Sara's heart ached as he walked out of the restaurant.

"Well that's too bad," said Barbara, "he was so handsome. Those dimples. I saw you looking at him, smiling and smiling."

On the car ride back in Barbara's Cadillac Sara sat somberly looking out the window at the darkness outside. Faint outlines of the branches stood against the stormy sky. Only a small sliver of moon dangled in the air. She pondered what she had lost, temporarily at least. Determination took the place of disappointment. If she could make progress with the case then she would be able to win Brad over. "I think you were right not to tell him, honey," said Barbara, "Nobody believes this impostor story."

Sara became reflective. "They are interrogating Bartlett. I guess that doesn't mean anything if he's innocent. I'm supposed to meet with detective Cole tomorrow."

"I don't imagine that's going to go very well either. We don't have to rely on him," said Barbara.

"If I don't show up then that will incriminate me even more. They will say I'm failing to cooperate. I'll just have to watch what I say. We have to do this the hard way, and I feel like we're running out of time. How do you catch an impostor? It could be anybody and they can become anybody," said Sara.

"We need some way to see through the impersonation and get to the real person," said Barbara, "We already know that you can't tell the difference between what's real and what's not. But Mariana, she's a finely tuned instrument. If she's talking to someone, and they are not who they say they are, she will know. She can sniff them out."

Sara thought it over for a moment, unsure if it would be the wisest course of action after Mariana's last performance. If Sara wasn't so desperate it wouldn't even be worth considering. "It's not going to be cheap."

"We've got the money."

"Then let's set her loose," said Sara with resolve.

CHAPTER 22

Now that she had been abandoned by Brad and had no idea how exactly she was going to get herself out of trouble, there was only one place to go.

"I need to go to the beach. You should come with me." She felt like she did her best thinking at the beach.

The next morning, Barbara wore a pair of brown over-sized sunglasses and a large white floppy hat as wide as a sombrero to keep the sun off her face. She also wore an ostentatious green one-piece bathing suit that called attention to itself like a siren. Sara had gone with a yellow two-piece that Suzanne would probably not approve of, but Sara was comfortable in her vintage swimsuit. She wasn't in the mood to be pretty, she wanted to be comfortable.

Sara had undertaken the task of carrying Barbara's beach garb, at Barbara's request. It was slung over one shoulder but it was practically a suitcase, stacked to the brim with lotion, towels, a couple of beach novels, and a frisbee. There were already several families in place along the beach. Several children had begun construction on their sandcastles. Others were wading in the calm surf. Barbara picked out a nice spot and Sara dropped Barbara's bag onto the sand, then rubbed her shoulder. Barbara reached into her bag and pulled out two towels, lotion, two bottles of water, a book, and sunglasses.

Sara laid back and closed her eyes, letting the sunlight pour over her body. She rested, though she knew that it was an indulgence, she really should be working rather than relaxing. Bartlett was vividly visible in her mind, though he seemed to be protected on all sides from any approach she might make. If she couldn't get him directly then she could build the case around him, until there was no way he could escape.

She felt the desire to swim tugging at her. When Sara opened her eyes she saw that clouds had blown in above her. The sky had been swept over with darkness as the sun was shrouded. A drop of water landed on Sara's nose, and a wave of rain spread from the background to the foreground in an instant. Beach umbrellas were instantly transformed into rain umbrellas. Mothers shuffled along to retrieve their children from the ocean, chased by the rumblings of thunder as the downpour melted away the footprints in the sand.

Barbara pulled an umbrella from her bag and popped it open, resting it on her shoulder as she watched Sara wading through the rough surf to go for a swim.

CHAPTER 23

She nervously glanced at the clock on the wall. He should have arrived ten minutes ago. Sara scratched the back of her neck, then took another sip of coffee. She had chosen an isolated corner of the cafe where there weren't any bystanders to recognize her and stare at her. She was also far enough from the other customers to comfortably raise her voice if she needed to. At least she wouldn't be caught off guard, she thought to herself, thanks to Barbara. The detective probably suspected her more than Bartlett at this point. He probably believed that the conversation she heard before Joy's body was discovered was the voice of a guilty conscience calling out to a murderer, the ghost of the murdered accusing the murderer, driving her to madness and forcing her to flee to the police station to confess her crime and be led away to her prison cell, a prison cell being preferable to being haunted by this crime. Why else would the prime suspect go straight to the police station unless she wanted to be caught, but couldn't bear to hear herself confessing her wicked crime.

The detective strolled into the busy cafe, weaving

through the busy waitresses and full tables. He looked healthy, handsome even. He looked refreshed, like he had just slept for nine hours.

"I saw the newspaper article," he said.

"Did you? Early yesterday morning before we met?"

"No, in fact, it was later in the evening."

She wanted to believe that he was telling the truth. She hoped to catch him off guard, and so she confronted him directly and immediately, "I already know that you are all after me. You know you can't keep a secret from me and Barbara for very long."

"I'm not after you," he shot back, "everyone else, on the other hand, it's a different story. Did you expect anything different from them? They think that court cases are made on assembly lines. They definitely have their eyes on you."

"At least you can protect me from them."

"I'm not saying that, but I want to make sure I have access to you before they lock you up. Not that you should be concerned. The faster we work, the better, regardless."

It was nice at least to have a man that actually wanted to be on her side.

"So what did Bartlett say?"

"Bartlett was...you can probably imagine."

"Arrogant?"

"Like you wouldn't believe," the detective smiled, "Almost like he was teasing us. It was just short of a full confession. He admitted that their relationship was not going well. The romance had begun to grow stale, he said. He and Joy had arguments and Joy completely disconnected from him in a petty way, she quit talking to him, would not return phone calls or emails. This was a couple of weeks before her disappearance."

"Even the devil…"

"What's that?"

"Something Barbara told me one time. Even the devil will tell the truth if it's to his advantage."

The detective continued, "A woman called him wanting to see a property of his. She was speaking with a southern drawl. Later that day as he drove up he saw you standing there." Detective Cole pulled out a tape recorder and laid it on the table, then pressed the record button. "Just let me hear your impression of a southern accent. Just do your best."

"That was Barbara on the phone," protested Sara.

"And yet you were the one that showed up at the property. I don't like doing this, but it would clear things up for everybody else if you could just speak into the recorder."

Sara was wary, but went ahead and cleared her throat and did her best Barbara impression. "Alright. Hay ya'll. Hay hunny. Watchall doin'? I can't talk like her."

He looked at her skeptically, then turned off the tape recorder. "Be careful. The police aren't the only ones with an eyebrow raised, according to the newspaper."

"That was Barbara too!" Sara protested.

"It's always Barbara, huh. There was one other thing that Bartlett told us, and I think you will find it interesting."

Later that day, Sara sat at the kitchen table with Barbara while Barbara ate some banana pudding.

"We've got him. Bartlett. He lied to the cops during his interrogation."

"What did he say?" asked Barbara.

"Bartlett told them that I had a crush on him, and I wanted him to be mine. He is so panicked that he's trying to make them think that I killed her. He actually told them that I was in love with him. You look like you still don't believe me," said Sara.

Barbara stopped, set her spoon down, and replied, "I don't know. Just because it's not true, it doesn't mean he's a liar. He's the sort to actually believe it."

"He knows something for sure, and I'm going to find out what it is."

She had to have Brad. It didn't matter if everyone else in the town mistrusted her, she couldn't bear the thought of him losing his trust in her, all because of someone else's lie. Sara was ready to get down to business and do what she did best: start from scratch. Sara's mind geared up, it felt like an old familiar car was being warmed up. The stakes were huge, her freedom was on the line. She would investigate, develop leads, and chase them until she found the criminal she was looking for, and finally get justice for Joy.

She set to work, following leads wherever they led, turned around at every dead end and created her own pathways. The normally crooked paths were straight and narrow. Ex-boyfriends, they were bitter but amiable, all of Joy's unpaid loans had been paid eventually. She quit a softball team; the team was happy to see her go. Rather than pursuing the regular thoroughfares of a person's life Sara had to go off the map completely. 'The murderer would have to eat somewhere,' she thought. The cashiers at the grocery stores hadn't seen anything suspicious, neither had the waitresses in the nearby restaurants. 'The murderer would have to wash up afterwards,' she thought, but there were no leads at the laundromat either. No pizza deliveries were made to Joy's house, so said the pizza delivery boy.

Sara knew that there was one man in town that had tirelessly staked out Joy's house on a regular basis. There was a chance he might have seen something out of the ordinary. If she wanted to get to him though, she would have to stake out the house herself.

Sara parked on the side of the road, at the wooded lot across from Joy's house. As she waited patiently for her quarry to arrive, Sara thought back to the first time that she met Joy. Two of the men that Joy was dating were involved in a corporate money laundering scheme. Joy was, Sara couldn't think of the word, then recalled it: an egalitarian. Looks didn't matter to her; she had a money fetish. She wasn't looking for a man, she was shopping for a lifestyle.

Sara tried to picture her face. She remembered her in the back seat, being chauffeured, so alive, wind blowing through the open windows, laughing at the idiocy of criminals.

Joy always had a high opinion of men. She could find a use for any man, and so she used every one that she met. It had been fun. After that they continued having lunches together and shopping. She was Joy's Barbara. It occurred to Sara just now that maybe that was the reason Barbara never liked her. Then again, Barbara didn't approve of Joy's conduct, her methods were fine, breaking hearts for a cause, but it was the fact that Joy enjoyed it so, that bothered Barbara. "The most important thing is for you to be yourself," Sara would say.

The person Sara was waiting for finally arrived. The mailman's car rounded the corner and stopped at the nearest mailbox. Sara watched as he filled up the first mailbox, then moved on to the next. Sara opened her car door and stepped out, ready to pounce. The mailman was only one mailbox away. When he stopped at Joy's she would only have a few moments to cross the street and casually approach him. The mail carrier placed the mail and closed the mailbox, then drove towards Joy's. Sara began to cross the street. To her surprise, rather than stopping right in front of her, the mailcar sped past, completely skipping over Joy's mailbox and stopped at the next house. Sara calmly continued walking towards the mail car. She needed answers. As she got close to the vehicle, before she could say anything, the car drove forward to the next mailbox. She walked a little more briskly as the mailman's hand reached out and placed a bundle of mail inside the mailbox, and then, as Sara approached, the car pulled away and drove to the next house. This time, as she was halfway there, she called out, "Excuse me?" She was answered by the rev of the engine as it accelerated towards the next mailbox. "Oh, come on."

Jogging now, she made up ground as she brushed the hair out of her face. This situation was yet another reason why Sara defied Barbara's orders and refused to wear high heels on all occasions, in all walks of life.

She thought to herself, 'He must have a two hour workday at this rate.' Just as she reached the car, he put it into drive and sped off to the next mailbox one block away.

It was starting to look like he was actually trying to get away from her, but was making a halting escape. At the next stop he hurriedly stopped and almost threw a stack of magazines and letters out of the car and into the mailbox. She saw it this time, he clearly glanced back at her in the mirror right before he hit the accelerator. Panting, she took off again.

As he reached out to shove the letters into the mailbox, one of them dropped to the ground. Panting, Sara reached the car and picked up the letter, placing it in the mailbox as she rested one hand on his car door.

He was young, and too scruffy looking to earn a place in her dating rolodex.

"What do you want?" he grumbled.

Sara leaned into the car. It was still in drive, but his foot was resting tenuously on the brake. "I just want to know about that house back there," she said.

"Which one?"

"The one a couple of blocks back. Turner." "I don't look at people's mail, so if that's what you're after then beat it." Sara didn't leave. "Maybe I'll look at a magazine once in a while, whatever."

"No," said Sara, "You didn't even deliver any mail there today, you skipped over it. I was just wondering if you ever noticed anyone besides her around the house, or any cars parked in her driveway?"

"Which one is that?" he asked. "Turner, Joy? I haven't even delivered anything there in a long time."

"Why not?"

"Uh, there was either a hold put on it, oh yeah, all the mail is being forwarded to her new address." He put the mail car in park. "Is something wrong?"

CHAPTER 24

Later that afternoon Sara entered the post office carrying a tightly taped cardboard box under one arm, with Barbara walking along at her side. "I think it will break, it won't work," said Barbara.

A line of people holding various articles stood staring straight ahead. Clerks stood in the stale air handing out stamps and envelopes and accepting packages. Multicolored stamps were on display on the wall. Sara and Barbara stood in the long line slowly inching forward.

"Has Mariana got anything?"

"She has, actually," said Barbara, "A restraining order from Joy's parents."

"That's good," said Sara, "At least she's been trying to get close. Did she find out anything?"

"She said the ghosts around them are starting to suspect Bartlett."

Sara hefted the heavy package onto a nearby desk and pulled a pen out of her purse. She wrote Joy Turner's name and address on the front of the box.

"Don't use your return address," said Barbara.

"I'm not," replied Sara as she finished it off and lifted up the box. "909 Cherry Street. The ghost house. Addressed to Matilda Broomfield. My kindergarten teacher. Probably a ghost herself by now."

The person in line in front of them was waved forward by a postal clerk.

"Explain to me what you're going to do afterwards," said Barbara persistently.

"The security system in the box has a battery hooked up to it, right? It was designed to catch car thieves. That's why there's a homing beacon on it. Now I've re-engineered it to catch a murderer. First, I give the box some time to get delivered to Joy's house, and then forwarded to wherever. Then, when I call the security company and report my car stolen they will activate the homing beacon and all I have to do is follow the police to wherever the package ends up."

"Then you'll have some real explaining to do," Barbara said.

"They will be too busy arresting the killer to worry about me," Sara replied.

The postal clerk waved Sara forward and she sat the heavy cardboard box on the counter and proceeded to purchase the fastest shipping possible.

The next day, Sara stood in a sunny parking lot wearing shades and a blue dress. The sky was a light shade of blue, matching her outfit. There was no sign of an impending storm. For now the coast was clear.

The nearby restaurant, Peachy's Soul Food, was busy with the lunch-hour rush. Customers were still parking and going inside to stand in line. Sara was a tad hungry, but didn't go inside. She reached into her purse and pulled out her little black cell phone. She reached into her purse again and grabbed a small crumpled piece of paper with some numbers scrawled on it, and then she dialed the numbers. The voice on the other end piped up, "Break-in security?"

"Yes, this is Sara Steinberg, my car has been stolen. I don't know what to do."

"Stay calm, ma'am. The tracking signal on your car is working. We are notifying your local police as we speak."

"What a relief," said Sara as two policemen exited Peachy's Soul Food and got into their respective squad cars.

"Ok," said Sara, "I appreciate your help, thanks, bye," and she abruptly shut off her cell phone. She then hurriedly got into the very car she had reported stolen. The two police cars pulled out of the parking lot one after the other and blasted their police sirens. Sara cranked the engine and followed behind.

She drove steadily behind the police car trying to keep at least two cars between hers and the policeman's, which wasn't easy because the policeman was going twenty over the speed limit. Approaching another car, she swerved out into the next lane and then swerved back in as soon as she had passed it. It didn't matter how erratically she drove, she reminded herself that she just had to stay out of that policeman's rear-view mirror.

The police car momentarily drove into the oncoming lane to bypass the backed up cars at the stoplight. Sara contemplated pursuing it, but stopped herself, not wanting to draw unnecessary attention to herself. This momentary lapse of responsibility soon passed and she sped into the oncoming lane. She steered around the traffic just as the light was turning green and had to maneuver through two collapsing walls of cars which honked as she drove between them. They were driving now on Brad's side of town. There were a lot less straightaways, more winding roads and sharp turns. The police cruiser pulled ahead around a curve and Sara sped up even more to keep pace.

As she rounded the curve the police car was nowhere to be seen, it must have turned off somewhere. She quickly rolled down her window and listened to the distant whine of a blaring siren, then she took a hard left onto a side road. She was able to catch up fairly easily because she had recently driven on these roads on the way to see Brad. As the police car rounded another curve two more cruisers pulled into the road joining it, their sirens blaring. They rounded another corner and two more police cars joined in.

It looked like the entire police force was riding with her now. They turned a corner towards the beach. Now it was unmistakable. They were driving towards Brad's house. Sara felt a tightening in her chest.

CHAPTER 25

As she nervously followed and attentively watched, the cavalcade of police cars drove past Brad's house and pulled into the empty lot at 909 Cherry Street. Profoundly relieved on the one hand, Sara still cursed her luck, "They marked it 'Return to Sender.' " Two more police cars arrived, blocking the road ahead. Sara quickly pulled into Brad's driveway, trying her best to look inconspicuous.

She got out of her green car and could see the policemen out of their cars now and beginning to rove around the ghost house's land with guns drawn. Suddenly a policeman whistled and the rest turned their heads. He was peering into the mailbox. He carefully pulled out the package and looked it over, then shook it, listening carefully. The policeman then scrutinized the front of the package. He activated his police radio and barked out an order, "Put a bulletin out for Matilda Broomfield. Arrest on sight. May be armed."

Sara noticed the strange new look of Brad's beach house. After running out of lumber from the wreckage of his neighbors' houses he had resorted to dragging long timbers of driftwood down the beach to further fortify his fortress. Gnarled and twisted, smoothed by weeks of being pounded in the salty surf, the thick limbs were nailed all over in functional decoration that added a folk art mystique to the structure.

She spotted him up on the deck trying to wedge a thick wooden pole into place. "And where's the rest of the Swiss Family Robinson?" she called up.

"I was thinking of Robinson Crusoe. It looks like his summer home." Brad leaned hard and shoved the driftwood pole into a tight fit and then stood up, noticing that Sara had not taken her eyes off him since she first saw him. He met her stare as he wiped his brow, "That's not the worst of it. I'm running out of lumber from my neighbors' houses. I can usually count on the ocean to bring me the wood I need, but I guess I've picked those bones clean."

Sara leaned against the driftwood wall and ran a finger along its grooves. "Well, it looks…"

"-primal," said Brad, as he looked down straight through her eyes. "It's born out of desperation, but there might be some accidental wisdom in it. I mean, these timbers are strong. The ocean tried its best to break them apart, but they survived. The weak ones were smashed into splinters but these were special. They know how to take a beating. If I'm going to survive this thing I'm going to need more friends like these. Speaking of which, is that a friend of yours?" asked Brad as he pointed behind her. She was afraid to turn around.

"Ma'am, were you driving this vehicle?" A tall middle-aged policeman with a trim mustache, consternation creases on his forehead, and an idle stare stood directly behind her.

She sheepishly turned around to face him. "Maybe," she replied.

"I'll be back for dinner tomorrow," yelled Sara as the policeman slammed the squad car door shut. The humiliation was dampened by the soft hope that Brad would not turn his back on her. This was before Brad shook his head, turned his back, and walked into the house.

CHAPTER 26

The handcuffs on her wrists weren't too tight. They hung
loose like bracelets, the way Sara liked it. She was sitting on a
steel bench in the hallway of the police station. They hadn't
locked her up yet. The officers were talking things over in
another room. That was fine by her, but she was itching to
make her phone call to Barbara before it got to be too late.
Dull fluorescent lighting washed out the pastel green of the
hallway walls. The police station was still active. Officers
passed her by, avoiding eye contact. Occasionally a criminal
would be led past, and they always made eye contact. An
elderly woman slowly entered the hallway in handcuffs, being
led by a young policeman.
"I didn't steal any car," the old woman protested as the
policeman pulled her along. "Put a lid on it, Broomfield," the
policeman said.
"Oh. Hi, Sara," she said as she was marched past.
Sara watched her until she disappeared around the corner and
then there was quiet again. A nearby door opened. A mature
officer appeared, his broad brown mustache was fringed with

gray, and his traffic stop grimace was set in the lines on his face. He held the package she had mailed under his arm. "The owner of this package is probably not going to press charges against you, so you're free to go." She stood to allow him to unlock the handcuffs.

"Didn't I arrest you for pole-dancing in public a while back?" he said as he unlocked them.

"Yeah, that was me."

"You need to start rethinking your choices."

Sara only stared, bemused. The officer handed her the box with the security device inside. She couldn't understand why she was being released so quickly, without any extensive questions, until the officer added, "Tell Barbara thanks."

As Sara exited the building she saw Barbara standing there learning against her Cadillac. Her grey hair seemed radiant, even though there were several large clouds hovering overhead now. She was smartly dressed in a long pink dress with frills along the back.

"The package wasn't marked return to sender," said Sara, lugging the package in her arms, "They didn't send it to the return address."

"What does that mean?" asked Barbara.

"They forwarded it to the right place."

Barbara suddenly understood the implications.

"I want someone who can give me answers," said Sara, "I want to talk to Brad."

CHAPTER 27

The newspaper bearing Sara's mugshot was slightly crumpled and draped across the table. She knew she wouldn't be able to get what she wanted from Brad right away. Plus, she would have time for Brad to somehow get into her debt and owe her a favor. It would be better to reconcile with him first, so that he wouldn't doubt her sincerity. She needed something from him. A couple of things, actually. Alright, several things. She was relieved to have an excuse to go see Brad again. She was usually able to find excuses to do things that she wanted to do anyways. He probably wouldn't want to speak with her though. She deeply hoped that he would at least give her a chance.

Sara knocked on Brad's front door, but there was no answer. Not finding him at home, she headed towards his workplace, the beach. She was surprised to see that the walkway stretching from the deck to the beach had been abruptly snapped in half. The last half of the walkway now lay in pieces strewn across the sand. Sara saw a small pile of two by fours on the beach, Brad had already reclaimed some of the wreckage. The jagged end of the walkway now stood five feet off the ground, more like a dock than a walkway.

The sea was light green and calm, the sun reflected in a thousand sparkles as it peeked through the clouds. The small sailboat which was stranded on the beach was still high and dry, though the winds had blown hard enough against its open sails to tilt it over even farther. It was not unlike Brad's house, stranded by the sea.

She saw Brad standing on the shore beside a small tide pool with a long fishing pole in his hand. As Sara made her way down the walkway she noticed that his fishing pole was not cast into the grand ocean before him, it had been cast into the small tide pool, and Brad was staring intently into it. An older couple walked past him and watched him curiously but he took no notice.

She casually walked beside him, "You look absolutely crazy."

He looked over, "Shhhh."

She said quietly, "What are you doing?"

"Waiting."

He subtly jerked the pole. Small ripples dispersed from the line.

Brad then wrapped his hands tightly around the pole and pulled firmly.

A fat silver gleam burst from the surface of the small pool, a great two-foot long fish arcing in the air and splashing back down. Brad fought back on the rod and reeled, saying to Sara, "Yesterday I came down here, I've never seen anything like it. There must have been something in the air. The fish were swarming. I was pulling them in one after another all day long. The weatherman said the storm isn't going to hit here, but those fish were running. My freezer is completely full, I left the rest out here."

There was another hard tug on the line. "I'm going to have to cut off the walk. It's like a bear with its leg caught in a trap and having to gnaw it off. If I don't cut it off it will take down the deck with it." After he said that Sara realized that the house now looked like a wounded warrior that had seen serious action, with wounds only hinting at the battles to come.

His pole was arched over and his forearms were flexed taut. He gently tugged backwards on the pole and the line abruptly snapped, and the pole whipped backwards. The tide pool became perfectly still. Brad inspected the broken line on his fishing pole, then he called out to the tide pool, "I'll be back later for round two."

They left the beach, Brad carrying his empty fishing rod. He climbed onto his half-demolished walkway and then extended his hand to lift her up.

"Honestly," he said, "even if you were guilty I would still like you a little bit. I would write you letters in prison." "Oh, thanks," she said sarcastically.

"You know, I don't think you're guilty, Sara. I just don't understand why you weren't more up front with me."

"I thought I could clear all this up before you found out, and then you wouldn't have to just take my word for it."

"You thought that wouldn't be enough for me?" he asked.

"I didn't want to put you in that position."

"Of having to trust you?"

"It's too much for some people to bear. Myself included. I wonder if I'm going to make it out this time. Usually there's some sort of light that I can latch on to, but I look around, and I try to picture the future and all I see is a dark mystery. Of the two of us, you're the lucky one because you know what you're fighting against. I tracked Joy's mail, it was being forwarded to the ghost house. Are you sure there's no connection between you and Bartlett?"

"The only people I have seen digging in that mailbox is him and you," he replied, "He always left in a hurry, but I assumed it was because he didn't want to talk to me. I didn't take him for a murderer though. Maybe he wanted her mail for some other reason. Did you really talk to her?" he asked, referring to Joy.

"No," said Sara reassuringly. It wasn't a complete lie, because she hadn't actually been talking to her.

"You said I was the lucky one," commented Brad, "Come here, I want to show you something."

The inside of Brad's house was in disarray. Bundles of papers were haphazardly stacked on the kitchen counter next to a half-empty cup of coffee. Digital radar images of the storm were strewn across his living room table, printed out in haste hours earlier. Brad led Sara over to the table and shuffled the colored images around and laid a map in front of her, "They're not sure exactly where it's going to make landfall, but if it follows this trajectory and makes a turn..." he ran his finger along an imaginary line from the eye of the storm to their present location. He then pulled out a celestial chart from underneath. "Look at this," he said as he pointed to an array of moons along the edge of the chart. "If the storm hits, it should get here at the exact same time that the moon goes completely dark."

"What's so bad about that?" asked Sara.

"No, look." He rifled through a stack of papers and finally pulled out a tidal chart. "When the moon lines up with the sun there's a new moon. It's completely black because the sun is behind it. When they are both aligned like that their gravity is combined and it pulls on the ocean extra hard and forces the tide to swell." He threw the tidal chart onto the table and moved closer to Sara, putting his hand around the small of her back. "The sun and the moon are going to be holding onto all that water, and then the storm is going to come crashing in on top of it. There have been storms here before, but never like this."

Sara had never seen this worry in his face before. It was disquieting. It was the first time she had ever seen him uncertain. But rather than changing her feelings for him, it just made them deeper. She wanted to comfort him despite the hard evidence that things were not going to be fine. Brad picked up the celestial chart ornamented with constellations and the phases of the moon, and he said softly to Sara, "That psychic, did she ever give you an astrology reading?"

"I don't believe in that stuff."

"This isn't superstition, it's science. The universe is aligned against me."

"I'm sorry this had to happen to you." He had been wrestling with this for some time, she could tell. One of the reasons that he was so receptive to reconciling with her was, no doubt, because he was under such duress and needed someone steady to depend on. She now saw an opportunity to have him in her debt, but it wasn't malicious if it was from the heart, she told herself. Life is something of a scheme from the heart, she reminded herself. She thought she heard the rumbling of thunder rolling over the ocean from far away.

"If the storm does hit here, and I'm not saying it will," she vacillated, "but if this house is vulnerable at all, and I'm not saying it is, but if you want some place to go, and I'm not saying you will, you can stay with me."

A dark scowl set in upon his forehead. "That's out of the question. I can't leave this house." It was strange that his mood would turn so suddenly, and then just as quickly his scowl evaporated and he returned to normal. The way he said, 'this house' made Sara think that here was more to it than just the house.

"I appreciate it, Sara." There was something off in his tone, as

if he wasn't being sincere, then he finished his statement,
"...but I think I will stay right here and tough it out."
"What do you mean?" asked Sara, incredulous and offended.
"You would rather stay here during a storm than spend a night relying on me." She was incensed now. He claimed that he was over her appearance in the newspaper, but he was misrepresenting himself, as bad as any impostor. How could he judge her, she thought, when she was wrongfully accused and he was the one being dishonest. She didn't want to believe that he would lie, but the facts were plain before her.

Sara looked out the window and saw that the high tide waves had already breached the first half of the beach, and were pushing closer with every undulation. A long wave broke and gushed across the sand, pouring into the tide pool. A fish leapt into the air, and no doubt glimpsed the approaching surge of water. The captives' liberation was at hand. A broad wave of white foam overwhelmed the beach and filled the tide pool until it overflowed. A swiftly flowing channel was suddenly cut through the tide pool as the sand eroded, and through that channel several large silver fish rushed out into the open sea.

Brad broke the silence. "You know, I was going to ask you before, but then I changed my mind..."

She could tell that he was about to propose something to her. She was flattered, and grateful for the opportunity to finally improve her appearance in the relationship. Her understanding was that relationships are built on appearances as much as they are on the actual people involved. They each have to appear to the other in the best possible light. If one person's appearance was lessened, say by having their mugshot appear in the paper, then the equal footing would be lost and the relationship wouldn't work. Now she had an opportunity to restore her previous standing. This was especially important with Brad's philosophy on shallowness in mind.

"What is it?" asked Sara, glad to see that he was opening up.

"I could really use your help today."

Sara wondered what he was going to propose, picking up lumber on the beach maybe, or hammering boards in place.

He blurted out, "Will you marry me?"

Sara's eyes went wide open.

CHAPTER 28

Later that day, a brown car pulled into Brad's driveway. Sara descended the stairs to welcome the insurance agent. She knew that if she was able in any way to help Brad get his house insured then he wouldn't have an excuse to stay in the house when the storm came. She might actually be saving his life.

She had to convince the woman that the house was strong enough to survive another storm. Incidentally, she also had to play the role of Brad's wife. What kind of woman was this insurance agent? Dour, judging by her prim pant-suit. She wore the permanent frown that comes with working in an unfriendly job. Sara thought to herself that this would be more challenging than she expected. The woman carried a clipboard under one arm as she exited her car and slammed the door shut.

"Mrs. Rowland?" She sharply extended her hand to Sara, who grasped it and shook it firmly. "How are you?" Sara asked politely.

"Yes, well, I've got a little business to take care of," the woman replied.

"I'm sorry my husband couldn't be here."

"Yes, well. You're on the edge of nowhere out here, aren't you? Must be kind of lonely."

"Yeah, still holding on though."

"That's good," she said as she held up the clipboard and began writing some notes.

"Would you like to come inside?" Sara beckoned.

"No, this is fine," the insurance woman said, to Sara's relief. Sara didn't want to have to pass off Brad's decor as her own. "It's awfully close to the ocean," the woman said skeptically as she continued writing.

Her scrutinizing eyes scanned over the house. "It's certainly an interesting looking house."

By the way she pronounced the word 'interesting' Sara could tell that she had some work to do.

"The foundation has been reinforced by these beams, you can see," said Sara, "it's as strong as a mountain. My husband did all the work."

"It looks like it's holding up well, all things considered," she said as she glanced at the ocean. The woman scribbled some more on her clipboard and then lowered it and smiled at Sara. "I'm all done here. I think I've seen enough. Sorry to trouble you."

The warmth of relief and victory ran through Sara's mind as the insurance woman backed her car out of Brad's driveway. Sara was thrilled that she had in some way vindicated herself, demonstrating to Brad that she was worth having around. She wasn't only good at getting into trouble, but getting out of it as well. What's more now Brad wouldn't have an excuse to stay in the house during the storm. Sara decided that she wouldn't bring it up at the moment, she would let it sink in first and hopefully he would figure it out and arrive at the same conclusion on his own.

She walked into the house, then entered Brad's bedroom and knocked twice on the closet door. She put her hand on the knob just as Brad suddenly pushed on the door, knocking her off balance. She fell backwards onto the bed as Brad stepped out from behind the rack of coats, "Oh, all clear?" He laid down on the bed beside her. "I look my best when you're looking at me," she said. He moved closer to her, staring intently, "It's from a perfume ad," she added. When he wrapped his arms around her she felt like she was inside a beach fortress with a barricade around her that protected her from any external assault. He pressed his lips against hers, and withdrew only to whisper in her ear, "Sara, you saved me."

"That one wasn't free," she whispered back, "Now that I've helped you I need you to help me."

"Anything," he said.

That was exactly what Sara wanted to hear. Barbara had been right, "Just wait a day," she had once said, "a man will find a way to owe you something."

"I'm kind of on the outs with the local bankers here," Sara said to Brad. It was an understatement. She and Barbara were unofficially banned from the premises.

Sara now revealed the underlying reason for her visit to Brad. "I need you to use any connections you have to find some information for me."

CHAPTER 29

The town's newest socialite sat at a window-side table in the country club dining room staring listlessly out at the ocean marina and casually overhearing the conversations going on around her in the room. She wasn't an official member, but as Barbara's guest she had access to all the facilities.

The dining room tables were all set with fine white linens and crystal glasses. The diners around her spoke in hushed, reserved tones. A waitress dressed in formal black and white came by to take her order. "What will you be having today?" she asked.

"Do refills cost extra?" Mariana asked.

"No," said the waitress politely.

"Then I'll have a red wine. What? Oh, make it a sweet tea then." Mariana had ascertained by the waitresses' glance that this place did not have an all-you-can-drink wine policy.

Mariana pulled out her non-functional cell phone, randomly pressed a few buttons on it, then held it up to her ear so that she could freely converse with the spirits without drawing attention. She watched the seascape though the luxurious wide windows, all the while listening to the club members seated around the dining room. The waitress eventually brought the sweet tea, along with the burger and fries.

As Mariana ate her meal she took in the ambiance. At the table in the corner of the room a man in a brown tweed jacket and thin black tie casually asked his wife, "Do you think the new tax cuts will pass?" "I hope so, she replied, "we could use another jet ski."

Behind Mariana a woman came in carrying a tennis racquet and joined her husband at the table. "How did it go?" he asked.
"I am worn out. I'm still trying to fix my grip. I might be getting carpal tunnel from all that swinging. Who is that woman?" she asked under her breath. The spirits alerted Mariana that the woman was referring to her. "Is she a member?" "I don't think so," the man replied, "based on her costume." They both stared at the green and purple scarf around Mariana's neck.

A cell phone in Mariana's pocket abruptly rang. She put down the non-functional phone she was holding and put the other one to her ear.
"Hello?"
"Honey, we're downstairs."
"Alright," she said as she put the phone away and lifted the non-functional phone back to her ear. Mariana finished her burger as she listened. "Thanks," she said into the cell phone. She rose to her feet and looked back at the table behind her. "She hasn't been playing tennis. She's cheating on you. Again." As the husband looked at his wife with a mistrustful glare, Mariana threw a tip for the waitress on her table and walked away.

Sara and Barbara sat on a weight-lifting bench in an

empty exercise room in the basement of the country club. They were at the prearranged meeting place, and were in the middle of a conversation. There were rows of silent exercise bikes and motionless treadmills. The latest contraptions designed to burn calories in the most futuristic ways possible were lined up against the wall.

Answering Sara's question, Barbara replied, "Because I don't want them to see you after what you did the last time you were here." Sara thought back to that calamitous event from years ago. "If it was so bad, why didn't they press charges?" "Because I personally campaigned the members of the board not to do anything. I had to turn in a lot of favors that day." Sara was astonished at this revelation, but not at Barbara's behavior. "I told you not to do that." "Well, I told you not to bring those men here but you didn't listen to me." Sara didn't respond, respectfully conceding the point. For every time that she was aware of Barbara saving her neck, Barbara had probably secretly saved her twice as many times. Barbara could tell that Sara was feeling down. "Do you want me to buy you a new car, honey?" Sara wouldn't think of parting with her cherished and reliable green vehicle. It would have to give out before she did. "No," she said. Looking around the exercise room, Barbara eyed one of the newer machines.

"When was the last time you exercised?" asked Sara.

"On purpose? Hard to say."

"Go ahead and try it out," said Sara, gesturing towards the machine, "It would be good for you."

Barbara eyed the equipment skeptically, "I forgot this place was down here," she said, "I guess a little exercise can't hurt."

As Barbara climbed onto the equipment she pressed the start button and several red lights lit up on the display. "What does this mean?" She hesitantly began moving her legs up and down in an awkward stepping motion, then pressed one of the buttons on the number pad and the machine began to chirp with another series of electronic beeps. She pressed two more buttons, which was followed by more beeps. "Why won't you start?"

As she jabbed another button on the keypad the foot pedals ground to a stop. A sharp pain shot up through Barbara's leg and she found herself suddenly losing her balance and stumbling to the ground. Sara was unable to catch her in time, and could only pity her as she lay doubled over on the floor.

"You really should stretch before you get on those things," said Sara.

Barbara looked up at the accursed exercise machine that was still flashing its lights and beeping.

"It says I burned one calorie," gasped Barbara.

Sara grasped her hand and helped her onto a weight-lifting bench.

Mariana breezed into the room, carrying herself so that she looked like a long-time club member. She held her phone to her ear and was wrapping up another conversation as she entered the room, "Alright, goodbye then. She shut off the phone and said under her breath, "Good riddance."

"Just the woman we wanted to see," said Barbara. Sara took a seat beside her and looked up at Mariana.

"Who were you talking to?" Sara asked.

"Destiny, don't you worry about that. The spirits have been guiding me around this town," said Mariana mystically.

Sara wanted to say: 'I noticed that these spirits always seem to hang around the best restaurants,' but she didn't dare upset the intuitionest at this point, so desperate was Sara for any lead.

Mariana continued, "I'm feeling a swell of spirits blowing through the town, but I can't make out what they're saying because they're drowning. The rest of them, they're not as smart as you would think. They are just as ignorant and dumb as they were when they were living, so I only have so much to go on."

"What have you seen so far?" asked Sara.

Mariana responded right away, "Relationships gone sour, or cold, or both. The frantic and lazy. Mistresses with husbands with other mistresses, secret plots. Loneliness, it's amazing what things people will let that justify. Wandering souls, worldly and otherwise. Consumers of every appetite. I have yet to find one person in this city that is not desired by someone else. There are warm households, dedicated mothers, and a surprising number of obedient children, the daycare in this town must be wonderful."

"That's what I hear," said Barbara.

"I still haven't found the killer yet, but you might be interested to know I have found the suspect. Word has gotten loose that Bartlett was called in for questioning. People are talking, it is echoing all over. The one thing I am sure of is that most of the people around here are convinced that you killed your friend, or had someone else kill her for you."

"Why do they think I killed her?" asked Sara.

"Because they believe that you were having an affair with Mr. Bartlett." Sara's face went white. She was incredulous. Bartlett's mistress. Of all the people. "Why do they think I was having an affair with Bartlett?" she asked.

"Why else would you murder Joy," said Mariana matter-of-factly.

'Oh God,' thought Sara. Their suspicions had turned into conviction. The town had already put together a sordid narrative of murder, love, and betrayal, with her at the center. It was one thing to prove your innocence and convince them that you were the victim of a simple misconception, it was something else to overthrow the intricate plot of an entire Greek tragedy that had already been performed for them in their mind's eye, with the delicious tragedy ending in Sara's clash with police and ultimate imprisonment. They already saw her as someone far different from who she claimed to be, an impostor. Even if Bartlett was convicted, the town would still be convinced that she was a part of it. The only way she would be cleared in their eyes is if she was the one to put him away. If the police got to him first then she would be caught forever in a cloud of suspicion.

Seeing Sara's distress, Barbara interrupted, "When people want to believe something their standard for truth goes way down. If they want to believe it then they need proof that it *isn't* true; if they don't want to believe it then they need proof that it *is* true. The burden of proof gets thrown around by what people want to believe. Human stupidity operates on impressions. They don't need evidence that you're guilty, they just need the impression that you are guilty."

Sara turned to Barbara, "Did you know about this?" "I've heard some whispers," said Barbara, "I tried to set them straight."

"That won't do any good," said Mariana, "But that is beside the point. There's one in particular that the spirits are whispering about. She's a good one at keeping secrets, kind of like Sara here."

"Suzanne?" asked Barbara.

"She knows more than she is saying," replied Mariana, "A lot more."

Sara's interest was piqued.

"So you think she had something to do with it?" Barbara asked.

"Yes, that is for sure," Mariana affirmed with a smirk, "you need to follow that one."

"She's throwing a party, and I'm invited."

"Sounds like destiny."

CHAPTER 30

Sara's hair and body were both wrapped in towels as she jogged over and opened her apartment door for Barbara. "I'm running a little late," said Sara. She checked her eyeliner in the mirror. It was just enough to give her eyes the fashionably dark mysterious look that Suzanne and her coterie admired. "If you're going to be late make sure you're fashionably late," said Barbara as she entered the apartment wearing a pastel pink top and light blue pants. Her hair had recently been done, evidenced by the lovely crisp waves of her white-grey hair.

Sara noted with surprise that Barbara was alone, "Where is Mariana? She was supposed to come with me to the party." "She is keeping an eye on the spirits at the massage parlor." "Oh, great," said Sara sarcastically, "at least I won't get kicked out early. She better be right about her."
"Are you wearing one of Suzanne's dresses?" asked Barbara.
"Of course."

Sara knew that Suzanne would be scrutinizing every little aspect of her appearance at the party. She could already anticipate being criticized.

"How old, this year or last year's?"

"This year."

Sara suddenly remembered that somewhere in her apartment she had an old tube of lipstick that she had purchased at Suzanne's store ages ago. "Where is that thing?" At least if Suzanne dared to criticize her lipstick she would have a good rebuttal. She also dug into a drawer and found a tiny bottle of French perfume that was worth its weight in gold. As she was picking up the bottle she accidentally sprayed ten dollars of sweet perfume into the air. She quickly lunged towards the hovering cloud of perfume and frantically wafted it towards her with her hands.

"What about your purse?" asked Barbara.

"It's worth more than the money inside it."

Barbara looked her up and down, "It might just squeak by," she said, "You don't want to put her out of sorts, you understand."

"I understand," said Sara, acknowledging Barbara's maternal caution that always manifested itself in these occasions.

"I brought something for you," said Barbara, reaching into her purse, "Take a look at this." Barbara pulled out a DVD. She put the disc in Sara's old DVD player and pressed play. The screen was streaked with lines of static, but then it gradually cleared away and the old beauty pageant footage came through.

Red curtains parted. A young woman stepped out of the darkness and stood in the bright spotlight on center stage. It was Suzanne in much younger years, the years that she was now constantly trying to recapture. She was wearing a gaudy glittering green dress that intermittently blinded the camera lens with its brilliance. She expertly walked to the front of the stage and she began her performance by clearing her throat and then affecting a British accent, "I positively feel like a queen up here."

"Wow, she's actually pretty good at that," said Sara.

She continued by affecting John F. Kennedy and Marilyn Monroe imitations and she ended the performance with a spot-on Joan Rivers impersonation as she ruthlessly critiqued the other contestants' dresses. "I've seen mannequins with more personality!"

Sara fast-forwarded the disc, then pressed play as she saw the crowning ceremony begin. An older bronze gentleman with slick black hair crooned an adoring victory song as the previous year's queen placed the glittering tiara on young Suzanne's head. A gorgeous bouquet of roses was handed to her and she smiled with her bright white teeth and began waving politely to the crowd just as the competition's runner-up ran up and tackled Suzanne, sending the crown flying, and the bouquet erupted into a cloud of petals. The beauty queen and her disloyal subject wrestled around on the stage to the horror of the judges and crowd. The screen suddenly turned to static. "She's got a pretty good right hook," said Sara, "I better watch out."

"What's your plan for the party?" asked Barbara.

"I thought I would get her to do some impressions. Then I'll see what kind of information I can get out of her after that."

"That's good. You've always got bright ideas. Make sure she doesn't suspect you. It shouldn't be you that asks her things," said Barbara, "because then she would be on to you." "That's going to complicate things," said Sara, "I need a surrogate. Someone to do my bidding. Maybe I'll work on one of her shop-boys."

"Your charms might not exactly work on them," said Barbara, "but it's worth a try. Barbara picked up Sara's purse and handed it to her, "This might be the last chance we have at this. Good luck."

As she drove in her old green car past the empty stores that were closed for the night, and the quiet oak trees that stretched overhead, Sara's thoughts drifted back to the previous summer. They had a good working relationship, her and Joy. She was beautiful. That was the least of her problems. As long as she had enough time she could get whatever she wanted. She was a good student, always eager to study. Sara had her sights set on three men. Each of them handsome, powerful, and ruthless. They each represented a separate organization in a smuggling conspiracy, and Sara wanted them put away for good. It was her ingenious idea, and Joy was eager to agree, the way to ruin them wasn't to launch an investigation of their massive and labyrinthine organizations, the way to go about it was to swiftly and boldly capture their hearts.

The relationships were carefully orchestrated, Sara conducted them meticulously. Joy used her looks to the fullest and methodically lured them into a love quadrilateral. Sara arranged the logistics, the scheduling, the shopping and preening, the progression of each relationship in concert with the police investigation. Joy would have been lost without her.

The unsuspecting beaus were strung along like marionettes until the climactic day that all three of them had wedding rings in their pockets and handcuffs around their wrists.

Sara was happy to take all the blame afterwards. It's one thing she had practice at. The men were probably still pining away for Joy in their cramped cells.

Sara and Joy were royalty for a time. They had gotten the job done, and more importantly, it had been fun. Sara wondered why things had taken such a turn for the worse. Joy was so dumb, Sara thought, it was obvious that he wasn't going to bring good things into her life, and she still stuck by

Bartlett. Sara even pointed it out to her and explained it to her, and put their friendship on the line over it, but still Joy chose him. In thinking about their escapades together, Sara realized one of the reasons she may have opposed Joy's relationship with Bartlett. After having complete control over her other relationships, Joy was finally in one that Sara had no say in. It may not have been Joy's problem, but her own. She thought back to the last time she saw Joy. They were at the beach standing in the sunshine. Joy was wiping tears from her face. "The most important thing is for you to be yourself," said Sara. "I am when I'm with him," she replied.

Sara steered her small green car into Suzanne's neighborhood. There were rows and rows of identical looking houses lined with hedges. Most of the neighbors' houses were as dark as the night, with only a few solitary windows illuminated here and there. Suzanne's house was easy to find, every light in the house was turned on. Sara parallel parked next to the other cars on the street and approached the bright house. Sara quickly ran a brush through the unruly storm that was her hair.

She could already hear the beat of the music pounding through the door. She knocked three times but the music was loud enough to drown out the sound of her knocks, so she went ahead and let herself in.

Passing through the kitchen, she followed the upbeat music towards the living room. As she rounded the corner she did not find what she expected. The living room was completely vacant, save for furniture and large mirrors which Suzanne was wont to gaze into.

The rhythmic pounding of the music fell to silence in an instant and Sara froze in place. The stereo system had been shut off, and now footsteps could be heard in the next room over, blocking the hallway which led to the front door.

She whipped her head around looking for a quick

exit, but there was none to be seen. The windows looked to be too difficult to pry open quietly, and she dared not make a move for another room for fear of a creaky floorboard. There was a closet door nearby, but she was afraid of the noise that might come from turning the knob. Her feet planted in place, she resolved to not move an inch, and she focused on quieting her breathing which was beginning to quicken, struggling to keep pace with her pounding heart.

Suzanne had set a trap. Barbara had been right all along. Sara cursed herself for being too foolish to realize the danger she was putting herself in. She could either confront Suzanne directly, or try to run for it. More footsteps in the hallway shook her resolve. She looked around for a place to run. It would be the unexpected thing to do, anyways. She stealthily moved over to the closet door and eased it open, keeping her eyes on the hallway. As Sara stood by the door, fighting against her lungs to quiet her breathing, the kitchen light was suddenly extinguished, as was every light in the house. She was trapped in complete darkness. The circuit breakers had been purposefully shut off. Suzanne knew she was not alone.

Sara silently stepped into the doorway. Not realizing that she was stepping into a steep stairway rather than a closet, she lost her balance at once, her foot slipped out from under her sending her body tumbling down the hard-edged steps which hit her body from all sides like punches. The side of her face smacked against the cold concrete floor. Her hands were wet with a viscous liquid.

There was a commotion up above. Loud footsteps ran though the house and a door slammed shut.
She looked up at the basement door at the top of the staircase but it was still open. It must have been the front door that slammed. Whoever had been in the house had fled.

Feeling around, she grabbed her purse and reached in and fumbled around until she came across that familiar hard rectangle. She turned on her cell phone. The bright screen was coated with blood. It cast a soft hazy red glow. She could see that her hands were also covered with blood. Thinking that she was too dazed to feel the full extent of her pain she turned the light downwards to identify her injuries, but soon realized that the blood was not her own.

At first, by the light of the cell phone, she could only make out the dark outline of a body, and the glittering of an earring. The jewelry was unmistakable, Suzanne's Queen Victoria diamond earring.
Against the concrete floor background Sara could faintly see the empty gaze of the former beauty queen and a knife's slash across her face.

Sara reached out and grabbed the banister and pulled herself to her feet. The soles of her feet wanted to slip out from under her as she felt her way up the staircase. She turned the light of her cell phone from the door to the hallway. She swept the phone around like a flashlight, wary of any other intruder lurking in the dark. She quietly made her way towards the kitchen. The circuit breaker box was hanging open on the kitchen wall. She reached up and flipped the switch. With a loud snap the lights popped on. The brightness temporarily blinded her, but her eyes soon readjusted.

Now that she was standing in the full light she could see that her white party dress was covered with crimson. She was smeared all over with dark red blood, it swelled and spread through the white fabric. With her body drenched in blood she looked like she had been the victim of a horrific stabbing, except she was standing there silent, aghast. The blood had not gotten onto her shoes, but it was dripping from her dress onto the white tile floor and running down her legs in red trails.

She stared out of the kitchen window, looking for any

signs of the intruder. The neighborhood outside was still and quiet. She left through the front door and quickly shut it behind her, and ran from the house, dripping blood all the way. She fumbled with her keys to get them in the car door. She was in a state of panic knowing that the intruder could be right behind her, ready to pounce, or a neighbor could be nearby and happen to glance out of the window. The thought didn't terrify her as much as the sound she heard in the distance. Police sirens.

CHAPTER 31

She managed to flee the neighborhood without seeing a police car. The ride back to her apartment was a frenzied blur. She was constantly checking her mirrors for any sign of flashing lights.

When she arrived at her apartment complex she parked the car in the darkest area of the parking lot. The parking lot was quiet. No one was around as she quietly stepped out of her car. The blood had dried on the surface of the seat. A car appeared on the road just across the parking lot. Sara stood frozen in place until it slowly passed. She edged along the side of the building trying to stay out of the full light of a lamp post. She stopped briefly to listen for footsteps, then quickly ascended the stairs until she reached her floor. As she stealthily walked along, the hallway echoed with the click of a door chain being removed and then the snap of a deadbolt being unlocked. An apartment door slowly creaked open. She ran ten steps forward and ducked around the corner just as a young girl in a short black dress stepped out of her apartment and into the hallway while talking on her cell phone.

Sara was silently hiding, and full of terror as if she were a criminal, the murderer herself. The desperation to not get caught had filled her entire heart with panic. She held her breath in, trying to keep from giving herself away until the clip-clopping echo of high heels faded into silence. The first breath she drew in was quickly spent trying to revive her exhausted mind, and so she drew in a succession of deep breaths before moving on to her door.

After easing her key into the lock and gently opening the door to her apartment, Sara stepped inside and then turned around and quickly slammed the door loudly behind her. She threw the keys onto the counter and walked through the apartment with only the moonlight through the windows lighting her way. She grabbed the curtains covering the glass doorway to the deck and forcefully pulled them closed. In pitch black darkness she walked guided only by familiarity and entered the bathroom, closed the door behind her, and finally turned on a light. She pulled back the shower curtain, turned on the hot and cold knobs as high as they would go, and stepped into the shower still wearing her blood soaked clothes. As the clean water rained down she laid down in the tub on her side and brought her knees up to her chest and wrapped her arms around her bare legs.

Bartlett had tried to set her up. He called the police to apprehend her at the crime scene. None of the other guests had arrived, only her. It was Bartlett the entire time. Mariana had been wrong. He had been able to fool even her. It would only be a matter of time before he came for her.

Barbara would be able to convince her that she was over thinking the situation and everything was going to be alright, but she wouldn't go see Barbara, not so soon, not until the morning. She didn't want understanding, all she wanted was to feel safe. She didn't want to sleep alone.

She wadded up her bloody dress and shoved it into a trash bag and tied the bag closed. As she drove towards Brad's house she threw the trashbag into a dumpster.

The slow, lonely knocks on his door awakened Brad. She knocked again with her fist.

A deep voice barked out, "Who's there?"

He opened the door and looked down to see Sara crumpled against the door frame with fresh tears on her face. He put an arm around Sara's shoulder and hurried her inside.

She wanted to tell him everything, all of her fears, all of her desperation and anxiety, they welled up inside her. She wanted to tell him the truth, but the fear of losing him, of having him recoil from her and slip away compelled her to become an impostor, and lie to the man that she had come to love.

"You can't keep away from me for long, can you?" he said. He knew something was wrong, because she usually had something to tell him and couldn't wait to talk about it, but now she sat mute, unwilling to reveal what she was thinking.

"It's been a rough day for me too," he said, "I didn't get the insurance."

"I need to rest," she mumbled as she crossed the room and sat on the couch. Brad sat beside her, but didn't put his arms around her shoulders again. Anger swelled inside Sara, she had rushed to see Brad in a panic, and now didn't know what to say or how to act. She could tell by his sharp breathing that he knew her problems had caught up to her again. She wanted to forget about what had happened completely, but knew she would have to get to the bottom of it. Her burden had multiplied and her future looked that much more dire.

"I cashed in a couple of favors, and it wasn't easy, but I got the information."

"Really?" said Sara, somewhat excited but not surprised. She assumed that Brad would come through for her. He shuffled some of the papers around and laid a sheet with banking statements on top. "You're looking at several transfers that occurred before Joy's death. The money is going from Joy to Bartlett."

Sara scrunched her brow, confused by the evidence. "Why would Bartlett want that money? He's got more than enough already."

Brad continued, "Then around the time of her death her bank account was emptied, stocks were liquidated. I think that he is the one that emptied her bank account. I looked at the checks. He had been doing it for months. I also found out a little bit about Joy's house being for sale."

"What?" Sara was stunned.

"Is that news? I thought that was why you suspected Bartlett. It was listed after she disappeared."

"Oh," said Sara, relieved to have another piece of evidence against Bartlett. Mariana said that Bartlett wasn't the killer, but he must have known something, Sara thought. If there was a real estate deal going on he must have had his hands on it.

Brad placed his arm around her shoulders and offered her what he could feel she needed most: rest. "You can lay down on the bed, and I'll sleep here tonight." Maybe, she thought, it would bring them closer together in a strange way, since they were both trapped in desperate situations.

"I don't want to be alone tonight," she said.

She laid her head against his shoulder.

He couldn't help but tap his finger on her nose as he spoke. "Then I'm going to be all over you. You are the beach and I am the ocean."

CHAPTER 32

The house was illuminated by the soft light shining from the morning sun that made the pale green curtains covering the living room windows glow. As Brad began to awaken he reached out his arm to put it around Sara's waist, but he only grabbed air. When he opened his eyes he could see that he was alone in bed.

The silence in the house pulled him out of bed. He didn't hear any chatter coming from the TV, nor did he hear anything sizzling on the kitchen stove. He walked through the house in his snug boxer shorts looking for her, but she was gone. Sighing, he went ahead and pulled out a box of ground coffee and turned on the coffeemaker to get it brewing, going about his normal morning routine. As he drew open the living room curtains he saw a figure out on the beach sitting in repose on the sand, letting the waves run over her feet and between her toes.

He walked along the rickety walkway and jumped off where it abruptly ended mid-air. He landed five feet below and strolled the rest of the distance to Sara, who was sitting on the sand.

"You're just in time," she said, "I was about to go wake you up. I was wondering, when you were a kid, if you ever used to build sandcastles right by the ocean and then do everything you could to keep the water from washing them away?"

Brad now realized that she hadn't been sitting idly watching the sunrise, but had been hard at work. Using handfuls of thick wet sand she had built a scale model of Brad's house. It came complete with scooped out windows and a seashell door, and vertical lines scratched into the surface to give texture to the supposed wooden wall. The few spiraled shells scattered expertly around the roof were superfluous decorations. "I know you like hermit crabs, so I put some of their shells around the house," said Sara. "It's a nice touch," said Brad. But what really piqued Brad's interest, as the ocean waves washed towards the scale model sandcastle, was the deep trench that Sara had dug around the perimeter of the house using a large seashell. It was a moat surrounding his sandcastle home.

The waves were already stretching towards the edge of the moat, just barely falling short as they reached across the sand. A tall crest then swelled from the ocean and crashed down, speeding a wall of water towards the sandcastle, but just before the water reached the house it was diverted into the deep moat. Another wave pushed forward and poured in. The rushing tidewater flowed all around the sandcastle, making it a small island, but it still stood strong.

Sara and Brad exchanged glances.

CHAPTER 33

Again, she delayed seeing Barbara. The first thought that occurred to her this morning was to find out what had happened to Suzanne's party. She had to find out where the other guests had gone.

"I'll be back before sunset."

She left Brad pondering the sand-castle, got in her green car, and headed straight for the Beauty Queen Dress Shop.

Sara was contented that Brad had enjoyed her idea. If he was able to secure the house against the ocean he might even be convinced to leave it during the storm, and ride it out with her. If she could only give him the excuse, she knew that he would choose to be with her. The anger and fear which she had wrestled with through the night had left her emotionally drained. She was as confused in the morning as she had been the night before, and desperately needed answers more than she needed Brad's companionship or Barbara's reassurances. She stopped by the promenade to do some shopping. It was only a pretense, she really just wanted to visit the Beauty Queen Dress Shop without arousing suspicion.

As she parked her car she saw several cardboard boxes stacked up outside the shop. To her surprise, the window dressings had been taken down and Suzanne's shop boys were inside packing up inventory. James walked out the front door lugging a heavy box in his skinny arms and he stacked the box neatly beside the others. She managed to duck into a surf shop and avoided being seen, though she could still watch him through the large shop window. He carefully set the box on the curb and then went back inside. "Can I help you?" an ex-hippie shop girl approached Sara.

"I'm just looking," replied Sara. She decided that it would probably be best to go ahead and buy something so that she would be inconspicuously carrying a full shopping bag when she dropped by and approached James. She looked over the beach trinkets on the shelves and pieces of equipment, skimboards and diving suits. She spotted one item in particular that she thought would be perfect for Brad.

The shop girl stuffed it into a paper bag and Sara headed out the door and straight for the Beauty Queen Dress Shop. James was carrying another hastily-packed cardboard box with lace spilling out the top. Sara approached him as he sat the box down beside the others.

"What's going on?"

Without looking up he murmured, "We're closed."

"James, what are you doing?"

As he turned his face upwards she could see that a streak of mascara had run down his cheek. "Oh, you. I'm sorry."

"What happened?" asked Sara.

"She's gone. I can't believe it." His face was drawn, its youthful vivaciousness had been replaced with despondent mourning. 'The news,' Sara thought, 'must have spread quickly.' "She just up and quit," he continued. Sara paused and did her best to conceal her shock and replace it with concern. The imposter had already gotten to Suzanne and taken over everything. James had no idea. He went on, "She said she was selling everything and moving to the Mediterranean."

Just like Joy Turner.

"Did you go to Suzanne's party last night?" she asked him.

"Oh, that?" He wiped one of his eyes and sniffled a bit, "She called me the day before the party and canceled."

"That's too bad," replied Sara sympathetically.

One of the shop boys walked by carrying a stack of dresses. James reached over and grabbed a stylish silver dress off the top of the stack of clothes and held it up.

"Why don't you take this dress, you look like you could use it, really. No, that's alright, I'll just tell them that it fell off the truck."

"I couldn't," protested Sara.

"No, I insist." A tear rested upon his cheek. Sara took the sleeve of the dress and used it to wipe the tear from his cheek. "No, just keep it where it belongs. You take care, James," she said as she placed the dress in his hands and left him to continue sullenly carrying out boxes.

So the impostor had disinvited everyone from the party except her. It was a trap intended just for her. She felt fortunate that she wasn't caught. Next time she may not be so lucky. As Sara drove her car away from the promenade, the radio station cut to a newsbreak which announced the untimely death of Suzanne Stripling, along with a word, "homicide." Afterwards, the announcer's voice perked up as she read the forecast, "The tropical storm over the ocean has picked up considerable speed. It's trajectory has shifted to such an extent that it is currently heading in our general direction."

With her stress once again reaching a crescendo she could only think of one place to go. She instinctively put on her blinker, and steered towards the beach. She wanted time to repose, to process everything that was happening around her. Hopefully, she would even be able to relax.

The sky was too cloudy for sunbathing. Anyone that was near the beach was only there to be near to the ocean. The strong wooden boardwalk stretched out over the waves. Its broad width gave ample room for several fishermen so that each one had his own fishing hole. The boardwalk was bustling as usual. Young and old fishermen alike stood along the railings with their silent poles hanging over the water. A child chewed on a corn dog stick. An overweight man with tattoos on each shoulder walked by carrying a baby, with a long-haired toddler following behind them.

Sara brought a lavender beach towel from her car and spread it out on the freshly trodden sand and then laid herself down on top of it and closed her eyes. The ocean surf was rough. The loud crashes of waves pierced the air. The waves rose up and curled and crashed in irregular frothy displays.

Her phone rang. No matter who it was, she didn't feel like answering it. She checked the caller ID. It was the detective. She let the phone ring again. Why would he be calling her now? Her pulse quickened. He had probably been to the crime scene at Suzanne's house. Sara considered letting the phone keep ringing, but didn't want to arouse any of the detective's suspicions.

"Hello?"

"Where are you?" he spoke quickly.

"By the boardwalk."

"I'll meet you there."

Sara's cell phone rang again. She glanced at the name on the caller ID. It was Barbara. She was probably panicked, Sara thought. "Hello?"

Barbara was clearly panicked, "Thank God you're there. I just found out about Suzanne. Where have you been?"

"I've been trying to get some answers," said Sara, matching Barbara's tone.

"Was it the impostor?"

"Who did you think it was, me?" said Sara, her voice rising.

"Just calm down. What are you going to do?"

"I'm about to meet with the detective."

"Sara, honey, why are you meeting with him-" Barbara stopped herself, feeling that she was being too critical, "just be careful."

"I will, don't worry, everything is going to be fine."

Barbara's tone grew soft, "I'm so sorry I sent you over there. I'll buy you a new car." "That's ok," said Sara, "I'm fine." Someone grabbed Sara's shoulder. Sara whipped around to see the detective standing there greeting her with a smile. "We finally got the phone records from Joy's cell phone. It showed that you had called her on the day that you came into the police station. It was being used on a daily basis after she disappeared. You were right."

These words came as a great relief to Sara. Finally the evidence was on her side, and her story was being validated. It would be enough to bring the entire town around to her side. "Is the phone still being used?"

"It stopped on the day she was found."

Finally he was acknowledging that she had been right all along, that she was not crazy, and that she was not guilty of her friend's murder, no matter what the town believed. At least she has been cleared in the detective's eyes, on this point, at least.

The detective scratched his chin, then looked away from the ocean and towards town. "Whoever it is, we think it was linked to the beauty queen case. We're looking for a serial killer now."

There was something about the detective's confidence that intrigued her. She could tell that he hadn't yet revealed everything he knew, he was keeping something from her. He must have some secret evidence that linked this case to the first one, or maybe there was even a connection to Bartlett. She wished she had Mariana here with her, but Mariana was probably getting a manicure somewhere.

"You've got something else to tell me."

"You're right," he said with a smirk, "I wanted to save it for the end," he gushed, "I've got some good news about the beauty queen case. We recovered a hair from the crime scene. It was matted with blood and stuck to the basement floor. The DNA lab is working on it. I don't think it will be very long at all until we find out who the murderer is."

CHAPTER 34

Tears swelled in her eyes, stinging as they began to overflow. Soft sobs erupted from her lungs. She didn't want to cry, she was forced to.

"My hair is my worst enemy. I am a dead girl. DNA. There is no way around it. They already have a copy of my DNA in the lab because of that incident with the Governor. It won't take them long at all to identify me."

She now wished that she could do it over again, she would have gone to the police right away rather than trying to handle the situation herself. Her independent streak had left her alone. There was no one who could help her now. Her independence had gotten her into even deeper trouble, but now it was the only way out. The conclusion was undeniable. She was going to have to prove that Bartlett was the killer before her time was up.

She had told Brad that she would see him again in the afternoon. She considered not going, but she wanted to see him now more than ever, partly to be comforted by him again, but also, as hard as it was, to say goodbye. If the police did wind up cornering her then Brad would never want to see her again. Before that happened it was important that she give him the present she had bought him.

As she pulled into the driveway she was confronted by a giant hulk of yellow industrial construction equipment parked in front of the house. The engine bellowed and Brad sat atop the monstrosity with a cigar jammed in the corner of his mouth and his hands on the levers operating a long hooked crane arm which he sent plunging into the ground to scoop out another load of sand. He then raised the clawed crane arm into the air and released a huge heap of sand onto the six-foot high sand barrier now surrounding the house.

"He likes to move fast," Sara thought to herself. She approached the giant machine but had to jump to the side as Brad swung the towering claw arm around and she almost dropped her bulky shopping bag. Noticing her at last, he quickly shut off the engine and stood up, the cigar still firmly wedged between his teeth. "What do you think? It's just like our scale model." It was obviously modeled after the sand castle Sara had built. In-between the tall sand barrier and the house was a deep empty moat that Brad had spent all day digging out. "You have no idea how much fun this is," said Brad, "I might put some alligators in it after a while. And a drawbridge, I need one of those if I'm going to make a proper castle. Haven't you always wanted to be a princess?" Sara had, but didn't say so, and didn't need to.

"Until then, though, allow me." He pulled on two levers and the giant crane arm reached down and gently came to rest beside her. She looked to him for approval, then stepped into the massive empty scoop. He lifted her up, as gently as if it were his own hand holding her. She hugged the yellow arm and couldn't help but stare down as he lifted her above the deep empty moat. The large shopping bag dangled over the edge. The crane arm stopped just above the deck and Sara lightly stepped off of the metal scoop. Brad then pulled on a lever to straighten out the crane arm and shut the machine off. The rumbling engine gave way to silence as Brad climbed out of the machine and deftly climbed atop the giant arm and precariously walked along its steep angle all the way to the deck where Sara was waiting. He surmounted the massive arm, then leapt and landed right in front of Sara.

Brad noticed the shopping bag tucked under Sara's arm. "Come rest with me," he said, and led her to the deck facing the ocean. They sat on two wooden deck chairs with the darkening dusky sky above them and the ocean immediately before them.

Sara surveyed the view in front of her. The walkway going to the beach had been severed close to the house. The boards had been dismantled and no doubt added onto the barricade wall in some way. Waves lapped on the beach closer to Brad's house than before. If the walkway had been intact the water would have reached halfway up its length. She turned from the empty view to Brad. She could see his strength in his eyes. He had been working non-stop, and seemed to be unfazed.

"I'm sorry this had to happen to you. It's not fair at all. The wind blows one way, and the waves fall a certain way, and then someone loses their home." "It's just nature," replied Brad, "That's the way things are."

"I got you a present." She took the liberty of pulling the present from the bag herself, and held up a bright orange life-jacket with white straps on it.

"What's this for?" he asked, with an edge in his voice.

"Just in case."

"In case what?"

"Hmm." Sara laid the life jacket on the arm of the deck chair. "In case you find your lungs filling with water, and you need something to keep your body afloat."

"When you said you had a present for me I expected more than a passive aggressive insult."

Sara was taken aback by his lack of gratitude. "Oh, it's not an insult, I'm just being practical."

"Because you think I'm going to drown."

"Because I'm worried, because you're acting like you want to drown." The sincerity in her voice was enough to prevent him from quickly replying with the dismissive macho saying that he had ready. Instead, he lowered his gaze momentarily, and looked back up at her with more softness than he had previously possessed.

"I'll tell you what hurts my feelings. If you want to know. You only bought one life jacket. If a storm hits you don't see yourself by my side. You imagine me being alone, and the only thing around to comfort me, this life jacket. Maybe you're not really worried about me drowning, you're just feeling guilty about abandoning me when the water comes."

She didn't understand why he had to be so difficult. It shouldn't be that hard for him to understand. He was asking her to put herself in danger. If he really cared about her he wouldn't be putting her into that situation, he would be trying to rescue her from it, the way she was trying to rescue him from it. And what was it that was so much more important than his life, more important than listening to someone who cared about him? Just a house with a beautiful view. He had to be crazy to expect her to unnecessarily risk her life. Unless, she thought to herself, that extreme level of dedication was not at all unreasonable from his perspective. She realized that his behavior wasn't crazy at all. He wanted her to love him that much, because he loved her that much. If she was caught in a storm, he would be there for her. He would stay by her side no matter what. It wasn't insanity, it was just love. An easy mistake to make.

"I'm just trying to help you," she said.

"You won't be here, will you?"

Brad's solemn eyes were turned downwards now, away from her face. He nervously used his fingers to brush his dusty brown hair across his forehead.

Sara regretted believing that Brad would abandon her if she were wrongfully accused. She wished that she could take it back. Still, she knew that she only wanted the best for him. "I have to leave now," she said, "I'm still in trouble and I have to fix it." She paused momentarily, "I don't want to leave alone. You're going to die here if you don't leave. You can stay with me for a little while, until the storm passes by."

"Stay with you?"

He seemed to sincerely consider it for only a moment. "No, listen," said Brad, his voice becoming suddenly softer and stern, "I want to tell you something." He stood up and put his hand on the railing of the deck, and stared out at the ocean. Sara rose to stand beside him. He turned to face her, and their eyes locked. "I want to tell you about what I did before I moved here. I try to avoid talking about it, but I want you to know." His brow was creased. He took on the visage of a much older man as his mood became darkened with world weariness. As his eyes glistened over and she stared into them she struggled to find the vigor that had been inside him moments earlier.

"I told you I was a stockbroker. I worked in New York city, in the World Trade Center. I was in the second tower when the first plane hit tower one. The people in the office thought it was an accident, they wanted us to stay where we were, but I knew what was going on."

Sara felt tears welling in her eyes and did her best to hold them back and she listened as he continued speaking with intensity.

"I was running down the stairwell and was knocked off my feet when the second plane hit, it was probably five floors above me. I thought I was trapped in there. The smoke started flooding in above me. I got up and I thought for sure that the whole thing was going to crash on top of me and I didn't stop running, and the floors seemed to never end, even when I reached the bottom and got out of there, people were jumping down to their deaths trying to get away from God knows what and I ran through the city in my suit until I got to the bridge. I looked back in time to see the second tower fall." Sara wanted to comfort him but the words caught in her throat. "That building wasn't supposed to fall," he continued, "but it buckled, it wasn't strong enough. After that I wanted to get away from it all. I wanted to go somewhere that was so peaceful that death wouldn't reach me, so I decided to come to the beach. Being here lifted me up. And then the storms came, and the ocean started moving closer. It's like the same thing happening all over again. I'm not going to let that happen to this place. I'm going to make a stand right here, and hold this thing up with my bare hands like Atlas if I have to. I'm not going to let this one fall."

CHAPTER 35

Sara drove through the cold night alone. She understood Brad's decision, his need for some control over the world around him. She even wished that she was up against a problem that she could fix with only a strong back and determination. She also regretted leaving him, but she couldn't help him with what he had to do.

After parking in the dimly lit parking lot in front of the apartment complex she walked past the large square dumpsters. They had been emptied already, to her relief.

She opened the door to her apartment, and as she looked inside her purse fell to the floor. The entire apartment had been ransacked. Kitchen cabinets were open, as were the drawers. Couch cushions were laying on the floor beside newspapers and decorative trinkets. The drawers of her desk were completely pulled out, papers were scattered around as if they had been thrown. The closet had been completely emptied of its contents and her dresses were laid upon the bed. Even the trashcan had been emptied and the trash was strewn across the kitchen floor. Whoever had broken into the apartment had searched every square inch looking for something. She walked around the debris trying to make sense of it, but there was no method to the ransacking, everything had been searched. Her books had been pulled from the bookshelves. Sara picked up her blankets from off the floor and threw them onto the bed.

The little red light on her answering machine was blinking. There was a message waiting for her. After listening to the message Sara immediately called Mariana. There were loud noises in the background as Mariana picked up, as if she were in the middle of a thunderstorm.

"Hello?"

"I want you to read my fortune."

Mariana paused for a moment. "Sure, I can do that. But it will cost at least fifty."

"I'll give you whatever you want," said Sara.

CHAPTER 36

The alley echoed loudly with a clatter as ten bowling pins collided together and fell to the ground.

Sara hurried past the teams of beer drinking bowlers who were more concerned with conversation and refills than with scores. Strings of blue lights along the lanes sparkled as the bowling balls slid across the gleaming floors. She made her way around the patrons snacking on appetizers at small round tables and found Mariana already helping herself to a full plate of chicken wings. Sara had taken a seat at the table before she was even noticed by Mariana. "Oh, hello there. Do you want me to order you some of these?" said Mariana with a smile, "No? And the onion rings are really good here. You don't want any either?" "No," said Sara, "I just want you to look at me and tell me what you see."

Mariana still held a glazed wing in her hand, "I see a lot of things, I always do when you are around. That is the problem. A lot going on with you. I am going to need some help." Sara reached into her purse and pulled out fifty dollars and sat it beside Mariana's glass of sweet tea. "That's a good start," said Mariana with another wide smile, her gold tooth glinting, "but I need something more than that. Let's go change our shoes." Sara traded in her flats for a pair of grotesque red and black bowling shoes. She had no problem picturing Barbara bowling in high heels if it came down to it. Mariana led Sara to an empty bowling lane, sat down, and told her to "Bring the ball over here. The one on the top rack."

Sara, her patience beginning to run thin, picked up the heavy bowling ball off the rack and lugged it over to Mariana. Her hands outstretched, Mariana took the heavy ball in both arms and then carried it to the front of the bowling lane. She stood with the ball held close to her chest as she stared down at the distant pins. Sara wondered if Mariana was just playing this game to distract her from her problems, or maybe Mariana was just as confused as she was, up against a dark empty void, and was stalling for time. Then Mariana lowered the bowling ball and placed it on the polished floor at her feet, then cumbersomely sat down beside it. It was then that Sara noticed that the clear bowling ball resembled a hazy crystal ball. Mariana's fingers stroked it lightly around its circumference. She stared deeply into the bowling ball as if it were a window into the heart of the universe. "The spirits are talking to me," she said in a solemn tone, "Their voices are getting stronger, their pronouncements are becoming clearer, the murky waters of the future are clearing up. . ."

She pointed into the hazy ball, as if Sara was supposed to see something inside. In the neighboring lanes bowlers kept stepping up and rolling strikes, casting puzzled glances at Mariana all the time. Sara took a step closer and kneeled down to take in every word Mariana spoke. "You will not be able to hide from the truth for much longer. You will wind up with what you desire most."

'Desire most? What does that mean?' Sara thought to herself. "But you are not satisfied with what I have told you so far," continued Mariana, "because you are here searching for something else entirely. You are keeping a secret from me." Sara nodded in agreement and smirked, "Listen to this message. I want to know if he is lying."

Sara pulled a tape recorder out of her pocket and pressed play. Adam Bartlett's voice began speaking, "Hello, Sara. It's me. I'm calling, just...I just want to talk to you. I'm making dinner here at the house tomorrow night. I thought we should talk about, you know, everything. Maybe if we worked together the both of us could figure this thing out."
Sara clicked off the tape recorder. Mariana did not blink. "He's lying."
"Good," said Sara, "I want him to try to kill me, I'm counting on it."

More bowlers were now suspiciously regarding Mariana and Sara on the bowling alley floor. Sara stood up, having received the information that she needed, though Mariana continued staring into the hazy bowling ball.
"The tape was not the only secret you are keeping from me," said Mariana.

Mariana slowly rolled the bowling ball down the lane as she got to her feet. She picked up Sara's fifty dollars and laid it on Sara's purse. "That one," she said, "was on the house."

The bowling ball clashed against the bowling pins which all cascaded down in turn.

CHAPTER 37

She walked underneath dim glowing street lamps, her hair
disheveled and her face cast in shadow. The surrounding
shops were vacant and dark. The thin layer of moisture
covering the street made it glisten. A flock of birds flew wing
to wing fighting against the wind, almost hovering motionless
even though they were flapping their wings as hard as they
could. Sara felt a sudden chill wash over her body like a
phantom flying through her as the temperature plummeted ten
degrees in five seconds. The birds simultaneously turned
away from the ocean and let the wind catch under their wings,
which set them shooting away from the storm and towards
some distant safe harbor. Clouds obscured the tiny sliver of
moon that was left, before it went completely dark and pulled
on the tide with all its might like Brad had described. Not a
soul was out at this time of night, and Sara was feeling the
isolation. She wouldn't feel safe at her apartment, or
anywhere else, until it was over. She knew that it would end
with her, one way or another.

Sara opened the door to the police station. Most of the

desks sat empty and dark, their lamps extinguished. As the door closed behind her the sound echoed through the room. She walked through the corridors, passing a droopy eyed policeman who turned his head as she walked past. The lights of the break room were still blazing. As she entered the room the detective was hunched over one of the tables, a cup of coffee in his hand as he looked through a disorganized array of financial papers. "Bartlett called me," she said. He looked in her direction and sat down his cup of coffee. "He wants to meet," she continued, "I'm going to meet him tomorrow. I need your protection."

"Absolutely. You're setting a trap for him."

"No, he set one for me, I'm just coming prepared. I need you to strap me with a wire so that you can hear everything he says."

He briefly thought it over, then readily agreed, "I can handle that."

"And bring some back-up. Not just three or four, a lot of them. I'm going to need them to rescue me."

"I can have six men there at the scene."

Sara's eyes were alight, "I'm going to need more back-up than that. I want Barbara in the surveillance van with you."

The detective hesitated. "Her?" He then nodded and acquiesced, "Alright."

The clouds were heavy on the sky. Though it was mid-day, Sara kept her lights on as she drove her green car towards Bartlett's house. She passed by the large white police van that was just barely passing for inconspicuous, which was parked in front of a neighbor's house.

She steered her small car through the grand open gates and drove along the cobblestone paved driveway past carefully manicured landscaping and a broad ocean view. She arrived at the roundabout which was the front entrance to

Bartlett's grandiose estate. White columns stood along the front of the house, stretching upwards twenty-five feet. The old brick on the house made it look more elegant than opulent. She scratched at the microphone which was taped to her belly.

The gutters that ran along the edge of the roof were made of copper that had recently been polished, and shone even in the muted sunlight. Seeing his yard reminded her of what they say, that he spends more on landscaping than most do on their mortgages. The hedges had been meticulously trimmed into perfect pyramids. She thought back with chagrin to the Egyptian cult that she had fought against and ultimately unraveled, but then that was a long time ago. She didn't expect this situation to be any less difficult and dangerous, and didn't expect the ultimate outcome to be any different either. She raised her hand and knocked on the door, but she did it so lightly that it would have only been heard if Bartlett had been standing behind the door waiting for her, or secretly watching her through the window. After an answer didn't come, as expected, she eased the unlocked door open and stepped inside. With the house momentarily to herself she took the opportunity to do some inspecting.

Her shoes tapped on the marble floors as she entered the room. Modern furniture was placed around the room, chairs that jutted out at awkward angles and a couch that was too high above the ground to be comfortable. Columns stood proudly around the foyer, more for decoration than for necessity, a common theme around this house.
'Joy would have hated it here,' Sara thought to herself. She could almost see her reflection in the polished floor.

The silence was broken by the sudden ringing of notes emanating from a piano. The keystrokes were struck softly and slowly in a melancholy rhythm. The melody echoed down the empty hallway.
"He's playing the piano," Sara whispered into her hidden

microphone, "I'm going to get closer."

The wood floor creaked underneath her feet. The far room looked to be a trophy room, those trophies being books. The bookshelves stretched from the floor to the vaulted ceiling filled with old, variously colored volumes. The multicolored books wall-papered the entire room. As she rounded the corner she was surprised to see that there was no one playing the black antique piano, the keys were self-playing of their own accord. She braced her hand on the railing of a stairway, listening to the eerie melody. The lone piano suddenly began to play itself faster in a crescendo.

"Go ahead, make yourself at home." She jumped, startled by the voice. Sara snapped her head towards the top of the staircase where the sound had echoed down from. Bartlett stood at the top of the stairs. "Don't act like you don't want to be here either."

Now that he had entered, the room smelt of cigarette smoke. He was not wearing his usual pressed khaki pants with a white dress shirt and tie. He had a brown sweater pulled over a dress shirt which was wrinkled around the collar. His face was drawn, beleaguered. Lines hung below his eyes. He looked as though he had not slept in some time. It made sense to Sara, with all that he had recently done. He had committed so many crimes that he wasn't able to impersonate a normal person anymore. The truth revealed itself on his weary face. He held a slightly puzzled look, as if he did not know quite what to say, maybe because he could see in her eyes that she finally had him figured out, after all this time. He finally settled on words that would suit him, "You look nice, Sara. You always did look good in white," he said, as smooth as ever. He continued looking her over, "As a matter of fact, that dress looks familiar. That's the one I gave you, isn't it?"

Barbara erupted with exclamations in the surveillance van.

"Oh, I should have known!"

CHAPTER 38

He was a good salesman. He talked her into it. He wasn't like Brad, Brad was a listener. Bartlett was a talker.

It was a whirlwind romance. It began and ended on rocky terms. He was wrong for her, and she knew it. That was part of the appeal. Eventually he had convinced her to warm up to him. She was swept off her feet. She was embarrassed to even tell Barbara about it. Barbara might have talked her out of it, and she did not want to be talked out of it. It was too enthralling being with Bartlett, being seduced by him. But there was a strain on the relationship from the beginning.

They were always preoccupied with their own lives. Sara was helping Barbara sort out the mess with the jeweler, and Bartlett was always busy marketing himself around town, trying to build a business empire. She wanted to see more of him, but had to settle for intermittent intoxicating encounters. It was a long distance relationship within the same town. They stole moments together late in the afternoons as the sun was setting on his mansion. He never once greeted her without a flower in his hand that was freshly picked from his garden. She never felt like she had a firm grasp on the relationship, and one day it slipped through her fingers. It didn't end well. He cut himself off from her as if he no longer existed.

In the surveillance van outside, Barbara was livid, "She was keeping a secret from me this entire time! It's so obvious now. She's sneaky that way. I ought to tell her-" Barbara grabbed the handle to the door of the van and jerked the door open but several officers pulled her back inside before she could storm out.

Sara ascended the staircase towards Bartlett. He stood motionless, watching her ascent. She wondered if he would seize her when she reached the top, but when she stood before him he merely offered her his hand and led her to the dining room.

Candles were waiting for them on the table, already lit and softly flickering. They were tall red decorative candles obviously meant for special occasions. Adam had never used them on any of their dates.

The lights had been turned low. Besides the candles, only the soft light from an antique crystal chandelier illuminated them. Paintings from the 1800's lined the dining room walls, each of them a still-life scene of different delectables, in one an array of limes beautifully rendered; in another a basket of fresh glowing white eggs. The red and blue rug spread across the floor looked like it had been acquired in some Arabian excursion. He had never bothered to dine with her in this room when they were dating. She realized now that he must have saved rooms like this for women that he actually cared about. There must have been other things that he had kept from her. Now he seemed ready to share them.

There were two empty places set at the end of the banquet table across from each other. Several silver pots were set on the table in between them, each filled with different gourmet food. The candlelight reflected off Sara's earrings as she stood beside the table.

"You look lovely," he said in baritone. "Why did you dress up for me?"

She allowed a half-smile to cross her face, it was enough to conceal her contempt.

The tension between them was thick. Despite the elegance of the dining room it felt like a boxing ring. Sara knew that she would have to work Bartlett over meticulously.

"Don't you like my tie?" he asked. It was the one that Sara had given him for his birthday. "I was thinking I might throw it out. I've got so many."

"All from different girls?" She knew that he was trying to tease her into falling for him again, only so that he could catch her off guard.

"I made you a nice dinner, Sara. Why don't you come sit down with me?"

"You're a liar," she said.

"You're right," he replied quickly, "I didn't make it myself, and you should probably thank me for that, but I assure you it is a nice dinner."

They walked to the end of the banquet table and he pulled out a chair for her. She sat in the chair as politely as she could, and then Bartlett, rather than sitting across from her, sat in the chair beside her at the end of the table. He then picked up the nearby empty plate and some silverware and placed them before himself. He was uncomfortably close.

Bartlett jabbed his fork into a braised pork chop and placed it on his plate. "Pork chop? No?" Sara scooped a spoonful of sautéed vegetables onto her plate.

"How is the wine?" he asked. Her glass had already been poured.

"I'd rather not have any," she replied curtly, "Do you have anything else to drink?" She only wanted to lash out at him and couldn't stop herself, she had been awaiting this face to face meeting for too long.

"Have you been thinking about me?" he asked.

"Yes, I have."

"I know you have. I'm trying to remember...when was the last time I saw you?"

Her stomach turned, thinking about Suzanne's death, but she coolly replied, "I think you were driving by that beach-front property."

"Oh, right," he said calmly. Did you wind up finding a suitable property?"

"Sort of," she said, thinking of Brad.

"I've missed you, Sara. You have no idea. I've been lonely ever since our relationship ended, you left a lot of emptiness here when you walked out."

"I'm not the one that ended it," retorted Sara.

"You pushed me away, I didn't want to end it but you forced me." His voice broke off. She couldn't tell if it was because he was telling a lie or the painful truth. He had her doubting herself and their relationship for the first time.

"You know, in many ways I preferred you to Joy. She never really appreciated me the way you did. I think she didn't love me as much as you did."

Sara wondered if it was actually true. She noticed that he hadn't even brought up the issue of how much he loved them. It was likely that he equally cared very little about the both of them.

"It was not perfect between Joy and I. I began to think that things were not going to work out. She always enjoyed the things I bought her, but she never appreciated what it took to earn them. My work drove us apart. I had a whole string of ocean-front properties lined up. You remember. She was distraught over it. She absolutely insisted that I not sell any more houses. I did exactly what she wanted but I knew that my work was not the real problem. I didn't want to stay on this island. I was going to take her away to some town in the middle of nowhere that nobody has ever heard of, somewhere quiet."

"You probably wanted to take her somewhere where she couldn't run away from you," Sara replied.

"I remember her talking about you one day. It wasn't that long before she broke up with me. We were talking about going to the beach and she asked me why you had been so attracted to me. She was worried, I think, that I had swept you off your feet in the same way I had with her, she was worried that she wasn't special. But I reassured her that she was special." "The same way you did with me," said Sara sardonically. "The exact same way," said Bartlett, without a note of irony.

He scratched the back of his neck nervously.

"Why did you tell them that I wanted to steal you from Joy?" asked Sara.

"I told them the truth: that you wanted to be with me." His ego was overbearing, Sara could hear it in his voice as easily as the words he spoke.

The piano could still be heard in the background, the rolling melody echoed down the hallway.

"Would you be interested in a walk down the beach? We might not have another chance before the storm comes."

"What are you after?"

"You don't have to be so defensive. I was just asking a question."

The flickering candles cast smooth shadows across his face.

"I invited you here for a proposal. My own investigation into

Joy's death has gotten me nowhere, and the police are clueless. I know that you have been unable to restrain yourself from doing what you do so well. I want you to share with me everyone that you suspect, and maybe I will be able to help."

"A proposal? You turned her family against me," said Sara.

"Her father came to me with his suspicions about you," said Bartlett, "He said you had always been a negative influence on her and had probably gotten her mixed into a dangerous situation. Once he figured that out then he thought about the fact that you had survived, and she had not, so he put two and two together and realized that you must have had a hand in it. Pretty good detective work, isn't it?"

"Fantasies built on suspicions," she replied, "and you lied to them."

"I can understand why you were haunted by her. You never could get over it. I know that you have been stalking me all over town, looking into my financial records."

His voice rose, and the slammed his fork against his plate, "When you couldn't have me it drove you to hate me, and you wanted the worst for me and everyone around me because if you couldn't be happy then not even your friend should be happy."

She wanted to interrupt him, but couldn't think of anything to say.

"We both know who is responsible for Joy's death. You're full of jealousy and rage, Sara, and it has twisted you into a killer."

She was painfully aware of the detective and van full of officers who were taking in Bartlett's every word, maybe even becoming convinced by it. Maybe when they came bursting through that door it would be to arrest her.

"So what was it, Sara? Did you hire someone to do it, or did you kill her yourself?"

Sara stood up and turned to leave, but Bartlett grabbed her

arm.

"What are you hiding?" he asked accusingly, "Why are you lying?"

"You stay away from me," Sara shouted. "I'm leaving."

She hurried through the hallway and down the stairs without looking back. Her face was flush and her heart beat rapidly as she drew quick breaths. She separated herself from Bartlett as fast as she could, though she had no intention of actually leaving the house. She went straight into his bedroom on the bottom floor in order to search it as thoroughly as Bartlett had searched her apartment. She opened the bedroom door and was taken aback by the already lit candles standing around the room, and the perfectly made bed with a red heart-shaped pillow sitting in the middle. She could smell the cologne that he had recently sprayed around the room. The speakers were turned on, as was the stereo system, they were primed to play music at the touch of a button. "I'm in his bedroom," Sara whispered into her hidden microphone. A small picture frame caught Sara's eye, it was sitting on the dressing table by the wide mirror which was itself framed by lights. It was a picture of Joy and Bartlett. They looked exuberant in the picture, both were smiling proudly. He had one arm around her and her hand was placed on his thigh. Sara picked up the frame.

With her free hand Sara opened the dressing table drawer. There were several articles of makeup, blush, eyeliner, and foundation. Mixed in, there was a tube of velvet lipstick from Suzanne's dress shop. But Joy never shopped there, Suzanne couldn't stand her. Beside the tube of lipstick was a single white pearl earring, identical to the one that Suzanne wore. Sara picked up the earring and held it in the candlelight. It was unmistakable. Bartlett could have taken the earring from Suzanne at the crime scene, but why would he take her makeup as well? Sara realized that the makeup had been placed by Suzanne herself. Sara whispered into her hidden microphone, "I've got the evidence. It's him. Come get me."

The door was thrown open with a bang. Adam Bartlett stood in the open doorway. He entered the room and slammed the door shut behind him.

His eyes were shot with rage. He saw the open drawer, and the picture in Sara's hand. The shock registered as a contortion in Bartlett's face.

"Suzanne was here," shouted Sara, "This whole time, you were cheating on Joy. That's why you had a falling out. It wasn't because of her, it was because of you. Joy must have found out," continued Sara, "she must have confronted you." As she took a step backwards her hand brushed by a remote control and the stereo began playing a classical violin piece. "Suzanne's business was failing. You were using Joy's money to help prop it up. That's why Suzanne was working with you to cover up the murder. Why did you kill Suzanne?"

"I didn't."

"Was it because she was going to tell everyone? She couldn't bear being an impostor anymore."

Sara dropped the picture frame onto the ground and it tumbled before landing upside down. On the back side of the frame was a small hidden microphone, which was recording everything they said.

"You're recording my voice?" asked Sara, "You've been recording me this whole time?"

He picked up the pearl earring, then stood silently staring at Sara. He slowly began walking in her direction. He was directly between her and the door.

He uttered only a primal grunt, "Come here!"

She threw the earring across the room. It bounced off the wall and landed in front of the door. As Adam Bartlett scurried over and seized the earring, the door was flung open.

Barbara stood in the doorway. A team of policemen barged into the room with their guns aimed squarely at Bartlett's head. His eyes went wide with shock. "No, Sara! It was her!" A loud crash resounded in the house as Bartlett was thrown to the floor. An officer struggled to pin Bartlett's arms behind his back. Bartlett, with the officer pressing on his back and forcing the air out of his lungs gasped out, "Help me Sara! Confess!" Sara was hurried out of the room, and was thankful that for once the police department had actually come to her rescue.

After her eyes adjusted to the sunlight she saw Barbara standing there waiting for her outside the front door, her hands on her hips, her bottom lip pushed forward. Barbara didn't need to say a word, but, being Barbara, she chose to say many. "Well, I guess you knew what you were after from the beginning. Mariana knew that you were keeping secrets but I didn't believe her. This is two mysteries we've solved here today, honey. I was wondering what that fuss was between you and Joy, and now I realize that it wasn't about her at all, it was about him, and so ultimately it was about *you*."
"Oh, Barbara. This is why I didn't tell you. I didn't want you to get the wrong idea."
"If you had gotten what you wanted from the beginning it would have been you that wound up in the ocean. Sometimes when you don't get what you want it's the best thing in the world."

Bartlett didn't resist as they led him to the police car. His demeanor had shifted to quiet resignation, and he shuffled along with his head down. Detective Cole stood by as they led Bartlett to the squad car. Detective Cole slammed the door shut, and then gave Sara a look that said he was happy to have the case finally closed. He approached her and Barbara. Bartlett stared ruefully out the window as the police car pulled away into the darkness.

"I hope he enjoys his new piece of real estate, eight feet by twelve feet," said Sara.

"We've got enough for a circumstantial case," the detective said with a smug smirk, "You won't have to worry about seeing Bartlett again."

"I found his network of microphones inside, that's how he was impersonating people."

"Those weren't his microphones," the detective interrupted, "they were ours. He was working with us."

Sara was floored. It didn't add up. How could he be working with them? She had to hear detective Cole say it again. "He wasn't recording me?" "Not that time, at least."

In the time that it took him to speak the words, Sara realized that she had been a player in the detective's manipulative game. He was after her at the same time he was after Bartlett. He was trying to play them off of each other. He probably bought into the love triangle narrative just like the rest of the town. The plan, surely, was to have both of his suspects indict each other in a double sting operation. Both of them were wired, and each one was trying to implicate the other.

"It was so hard to figure out which one of you was guilty," he said, "I knew I wouldn't get to the bottom of it without all three of us."

So he had been lying to her the entire time, Sara thought to herself. That's why he kept her close, so that he could find some justification for arresting her. Every conversation was really an interrogation, he was always probing for evidence, and it wasn't just the conversations.

"You were the ones that destroyed my apartment."

"Our guys are not very tidy. Sorry about that. You understand, right?"

Sara returned a look that made it clear that she was not in the mood to be understanding.

"I knew Bartlett had been cheating on Joy, but I thought it was with you."

"Very flattering," said Sara sarcastically, "I'm surprised you needed my help at all. You always make it so hard to say goodbye."

"Yes. I need a vacation. Maybe I'll start spending more time at the beach. Maybe I'll see you there," he added.

"Someone like you never finds time for a vacation," said Barbara.

"It's a sign of the times. You can't be too careful these days, you don't know who to trust. At least we got the job done."

"We expect to collect the reward that Bartlett put up," said Barbara

"I'm sure it won't be a problem," the detective responded, "as long as you have a sympathetic judge."

"Oh lord, we'll have to see about that."

Detective Cole strolled away, rejoining the bustling policemen.

Sara pulled out her cell phone and called Brad. He answered quickly, "Hello?"

"I did it," said Sara, relieved, "I caught him."

"That's incredible. You know I want to see you. Come over here."

Part of her wanted to. "I can't," said Sara, "You know I can't."

"In sunnier skies then," he replied, "Take care."

"I will. You too," she said as she turned off her cell phone.

"We'll have to call this one a draw," Barbara said to Sara, "we were both right, it was Bartlett and Suzanne."

"I couldn't have done it without your help," said Sara.

"You look like you could use a drink, honey," said Barbara, "I'll bring one to the beach tomorrow."

"It's supposed to be raining tomorrow," said Sara.

"Oh, right, I almost forgot."

"I'll give you a call to check up on you," said Sara.

"Ok honey, and Sara, I'm proud of you."

CHAPTER 39

Sara slept in the next morning. The clouds outside kept the sun off of her eyes. Now that one storm was over there was just one more to worry about She picked up the remote and clicked on the television. The weather woman was standing outside on the street, the wind blowing her red hair across her head, a microphone clenched in her hand, "...currently at twenty knots, with winds expected to reach seventy before the night is out, so make sure you are in a safe location with enough supplies to last you..." Sara opened up her empty cupboard, looked around inside, then pulled a flashlight out of a drawer and tried to turn it on twice before giving up and throwing it back into the drawer. She would have to call Brad and invite him to ride the storm out with her. Now that the case was wrapped up and he had time to change his opinion of her, maybe he would be less hesitant to devote himself to her. Regardless, she would ride out the storm with the relaxation that she deserved. Even if the power went out for days it would only give her more time to curl up nice and cozy in her bed. Then when the storm passed she would trade her bed for a beach chair and do the same thing in the bright sunlight. She went through recipes in her mind trying to plan out her mood ahead of time, which was a much easier task now that her troubles were over. It would be a chili stew that would warm up a rainy day.

Sara's Storm Chili
2 ½ lbs hamburger meat
1 large onion, chopped
add meat and onion, put it in a pot on medium, cook until brown
Add 1 Tbs of flour and stir
1 heaping Tbs of Chile Powder
2 cans sliced tomatoes
3 cans light red kidney beans
add ½ tsp garlic salt
Cover and cook for 2 hours, first bring it to a boil, then simmer
served with raw diced onions on top

She picked up her purse and keys and left in search of supplies even though the sea winds were picking up and the limbs of the twisted oaks were being tossed back and forth in light upheaval.

The streets were busy with last-minute shoppers like Sara. She had to drive through the parking lot twice to find a parking space. Outside one of the storefronts the old woman seated on the green bench was wearing a flowing yellow dress which drifted with the wind, and a broad light-green hat which complemented the green bench perfectly. The woman was looking over her newspaper as usual, holding it in place against the breeze. Sara was now actually happy about the recent news. She caught the old woman's glance and cheerily said, "Hello."

The old woman smiled back and replied, "Did you hear, someone confessed to the murder."

"Yeah, I actually did."

"Well, that's a relief is all I can say."

"Yeah, I think that's the perfect word for it, relief," said Sara, agreeing heartily, "One less thing to worry about."

"That sounds about right, considering what I've heard about that girl."

Sara stopped, "Who?"

"Oh," said the woman, "the killer was some local girl…Sara Steinberg."

Sara snatched the newspaper from the old woman and read the headline: "Killer Confession."

She rapidly scanned through the article, "Sara Steinberg has called the Daily and issued a full confession, which we have on tape."

'A confession? How? How did he get my voice?' she wondered. She glanced over the rest of the article, "authorities notified. . . innocent man accused. . . suspect is considered armed and dangerous."

The old woman noticed Sara's panicked expression. She added as an afterthought, "I wonder if that's the same pole-dancing Sara Steinberg."

A light drizzle then began to rain down. The woman looked upwards, then wrapped her heavy green coat around her and picked up her umbrella, "I don't blame you," she said, "I'm a bit worried myself. She could be anywhere around here. Well, don't worry too much. They'll catch her before the day is out I'm sure." She then popped open her bright green umbrella and walked off.

CHAPTER 40

Her stomach was in knots. She was guilty, of accusing an innocent man. She fumbled with the keys before she was able to get them in the car door. Nervous energy was coursing through her body. She had a mild headache, stress strained every thought. 'Bartlett was innocent. No, Bartlett could be innocent. He might still be guilty, but he's working with someone else.' She got into the car and slammed the door shut. 'Who would want to have me imprisoned? Maybe that doesn't matter, maybe they are insane. I've been looking in the wrong place because I've been trying to find someone reasonable. The important question is who could have pulled this off?'

It wasn't Bartlett. It wasn't him at all. She realized she had been wrong from the beginning. As she sat in the parking lot it suddenly became clear to Sara who was responsible for the perfect impersonations. It was a person who had access to secretive surveillance equipment. It had to be someone in the police department. It would mean serious trouble if it was a policeman, knowing how they stick together. It meant it would be her versus the entire police force. And there was only one policeman that had been trying to have her convicted from the very beginning.

Detective Cole had access to that equipment the entire time, he could have easily wired himself and then used his authority to get close to anyone he wanted. Most of his job consisted of interviewing people, even those who didn't want to speak to him, it was the perfect cover for capturing their voice. She thought back to all of the conversations they had shared.

From the beginning he saw that she had been close to Joy, so he decided that she was the perfect person to pin the crime on. Then when she came into the police station panicked and disoriented he must have been secretly thrilled, because it was the perfect time to put his plan into motion. He wanted to accuse the first person who would inevitably come forward, telling a preposterous story about having talked with Joy. The story would sound so outlandish that it wouldn't be hard to convince a jury that he had found the killer. First, he tried to make her look crazy by having her put in a straight jacket. Then he leaked information about the case to the newspaper editor so that the entire town of potential jurors would think she was guilty. It was why the police had arrived at Suzanne's house so shortly after the murder, he had radioed it in. Now he was closing the case around her so that she could not escape.

The rain began beating against the windshield in sheets with intermittent wind gusts.

She was instinctively driving back towards her apartment but came to her senses and took the very next right turn, driving aimlessly now until she could figure out what to do next. She was completely without a sense of direction. In her desperation she thought that Mariana could somehow tell her what was going on. She pulled out her cell phone and clicked on Mariana's number.

"Sara, child?"

"Mariana."

"The police. They are closing in on you."

"How could you know that?" asked Sara incredulously.

"The police scanner," said Mariana.

Sara quickly ended the call and then hit the speed-dial for Barbara's cell phone. After two rings she answered, "Hello?"

"Barbara, it's me."

"The police will not leave me alone, honey. What in the world did you do?"

"I was set up. It wasn't Bartlett, he's innocent."

"Wait, is this the real Sara?"

"Of course it is."

"Running won't get you anywhere, you know that."

"I need your help," pleaded Sara, "it was the detective."

Sara could feel the icy sting of emotional claustrophobia as the world closed in around her.

"Him? Honey, just turn yourself in, I'll sort it all out."

"Barbara-" In the rear view mirror she could see a pair of bright blue lights shining through the rain, and approaching fast. "Hang on." Sara threw the phone on the passenger seat and glanced back at the police car, which loudly blared its siren. She pressed the brakes and pulled off to the side of the road. The flashing blue lights got brighter and the siren grew louder as the police car approached. Sara breathed heavily as the car pulled over and slowly stopped behind her.

The policeman jumped out of his vehicle, weapon drawn. Sara picked up the phone, "Are you still there?" "Put your hands in the air!" the policeman shouted. Sara raised her free hand as Barbara said calmly, "Do what he says, Sara." Sara threw the phone down and hit the accelerator. The policeman shouted into his radio as he ran into his car and put it into drive.

The sheets of water turned her windshield into a hazy lens. A broad green blur in front of her slowly turned from yellow to red. Sara kept her foot on the accelerator and weaved through vague brown and black geometric shapes. She glanced in her rear-view mirror, the blue lights had multiplied, and the blare of sirens grew. She wanted to race straight over to Barbara so they could face this together, but Barbara's house would the be the first place they would look. She wished she could retreat to some impenetrable fortress. 'Of course,' she thought to herself as she scrolled through the numbers on her cell phone until she reached Brad's. It was ironic. His house was now the safest place on the entire island, given her situation.

She steered through a watery curve and her tires briefly hydroplaned, the wheels spun and the vehicle slid sideways. She held her bearing and the wheels quickly caught and the car sped around the curve. She dialed Brad's number. As soon as he picked up the phone she began talking, "I'm coming over there. Is the house safe?"
"I knew you couldn't abandon me!" He was absolutely ebullient, "Come on! We're going to beat this thing!"

She turned onto a side street, then made another immediate turn. She knew the mazes of these side streets well, and they were probably not a patrol car's normal beat. The number of blue lights behind her diminished. She turned back towards the main road, then off onto another suburb. To the police it would have looked like she was turning at random, but she was actually inching her way closer to Brad's house, and she was getting close. She navigated through several more blocks until she had put a sizable distance between herself and her pursuers, and she closed in on Brad's house.

A pair of blue lights behind her spun sideways across the road, the rest continued the pursuit. Her mind reeled to find some way to make sure she was talking with the real Brad.

"What's your favorite animal?" she sputtered.

"What?"

Silence followed. Her breath drew deep, until she heard the words, "Hermit crab."

"I'm on my way there." She hit the accelerator.

CHAPTER 41

The clouds poured themselves over the town. Heaven and Earth were joined with swirling wind and water. She drove half blind. The rain refilled her windshield as soon as the windshield wipers passed by.

At last she managed to reach the familiar neighborhood. She guided her car to Brad's driveway. She could already hear the waves hitting against the house. The sound of police sirens was quickly drowned out by the whistling wind. She parked beside Brad's blue truck so that it would hide her car from the street. The oaks were roughly swaying with the wind. The moat surrounding the house was now full of frothy seawater which sloshed around as each new wave poured into it. She got out of her car and looked around for some way past the moat and into the house.

When she looked closer she saw that across the span between the six-foot sand barrier and the back door, Brad had built a rickety drawbridge out of a motley assortment of lumber, no doubt desperately scavenged from all over the beach. She carefully walked up the strange swaying bridge.

The moat flowed with rushing seawater underneath.

Following the dull thud of hammer hitting wood, she made her way up to the deck, only the floorboards of the deck had been completely removed, leaving only the support joists, and Brad lay in the middle of it, his legs in the air, his thighs spread apart gripping the edges of the joists of the deck. He hung upside down underneath, shirtless, steel nails held in the grip of his bite, his arm swinging backwards and forwards, slamming nails into the wooden barricade protecting his home as wave after massive wave crashed against his home and sprayed salty water into his hair and eyes. He would have been drenched in sweat if he hadn't been awash in seawater. She held on to the railing along the edge of the deck and made her way around the empty spaces.

He saw Sara standing above him, rain matting her hair. He pulled himself up and laid against the remaining decking. "God, I feel like the last man on Earth out here, I'm single-handedly trying to stop the end of the world." He rose to his feet and put his hands on her shoulders. "How are you?"
"I'm just fine, how are you?"
"Tired. Why don't you dry off and make us some hot tea. I'll be there in a minute."

She had come to the right place. If anyone could protect her from the detective and hold back an entire police force it was this man. Sara's eyes brightened and she turned to go inside but Brad pulled her back around and gave her a deep kiss as they stood there in the rain.

CHAPTER 42

She sat her purse on the counter in the kitchen. Through the
doorway to the bedroom she could see Brad's laptop. A
satellite weather image of the town was on display, a giant red
blob was covering almost every bit of the screen. She looked
around in the cabinets and found a teapot, and then tried out
the water faucet, thankfully it worked, and filled the teapot
with water. Rain intermittently tapped on the windows. She
grabbed three teabags out of the cabinet and dunked them in,
and cranked up the heat. She could hear the thump of Brad's
hammer beating against the house. Her heartbeat increased.
She had doubted him before, but seeing him holding that
hammer in the rain made her into a believer. Brad really could
hold back the ocean if he wanted to. He would work
relentlessly, night and day if he had to.

    The methodic hammering outside ceased. Sara glanced
out the window at the rain smothered deck but Brad was
nowhere to be seen. The space in the deck where Brad had
been hanging was now empty. Sara froze in place. The only
movement outside was from the ocean spray splashing up.

She immediately ran to the door. It hadn't been too long, she thought she could reach him before he went under, even if he was unconscious. She pulled the door open and Brad was standing in front of her sopping wet, a confident grin on his face. She looked up at him, "The tea is on the stove," she said. He put a wet arm around her and they entered the kitchen together.

Water dripped from his darkened brown hair and ran down his strong jawline. He wiped his strong forearm across his brow and stood in front of her as the tea kettle warmed up behind her. "It looks sunny from where I'm standing, sunshine. I want you to know," he said, "that coming here to be with me is the greatest thing that any girl has done for me." Sara averted her gaze in an attempt to hide her shame. Once again, she would keep a secret from him. This wasn't the right time to tell him, she convincingly told herself. Brad was still ebullient, "Is the tea going? Good. I want to check the radar again. It looks like I was right, it's going to be an all-nighter."

He pulled the bedroom door open and walked in, kneeling down by the edge of his bed and staring at the fuzzy colorful blobs on the computer screen. Sara stood behind him, looking over his shoulder at the slowly moving mass of multicolored clouds on the radar screen.

The phone rang loudly. Brad glanced back. "Who would be calling?" Sara feared that it was the police desperately trying to ascertain her whereabouts. She dearly hoped that Brad would be too distracted by the weather to bother answering the phone. The phone rang again. "Would you get that for me?" Brad asked. Sara didn't move. The phone rang again. "It's probably just some evacuation call," said Sara a bit nervously. The phone rang again. Brad looked back at her curiously. The phone rang again. "Yeah," he said as he turned back around. Then the answering machine picked up. Sara had forgotten about the answering machine. "Hey, this is Brad, leave a message."

A familiar voice came from the machine, "Hello, this is detective Cole." Sara tensed up. "I think you will be able to help me with a case I am working on. I'm sorry to be calling you so late. I wanted to ask you a few questions in reference to your late husband Brad. I'll try to reach you another time. Goodbye."

A cold wave of confusion swept over her.

'Late husband Brad? Brad is dead?'

CHAPTER 43

She furiously calculated through it in her mind as Brad stood next to her, towering over her. She struggled to cope with his death, quickly moving from denial to anger. If Brad was impersonating his wife then she must have died without anyone knowing. But why was Brad pretending to be dead? It was all part of an insurance scheme. The insurance woman that came to Brad's house wasn't there because of house insurance, she was there because of life insurance that was being paid out on Brad. He was at the beach living off of his own death. Brad didn't just have Sara playing the role of his wife, she was acting as his widow. 'Brad tricked us both. No wonder the lady was so suspicious,' Sara thought, 'And Brad's actual wife, something must have happened to her.' Sara didn't want to think about it.

"But why would detective Cole be calling her? What does he want with you?" demanded Sara.

"I don't know," replied Brad coldly.

The lab results. They must have come in. Brad's DNA had shown up in the database. It was him. He was the one, this entire time.

She could feel him staring at her, watching her realize the truth. His breath quickened. She turned quickly towards the door and two strong hands seized her from behind. She flung the back of her hand against his face and his grip loosened. For the first time she could see terror in his eyes.

She pushed him away from her. He reached out and grabbed her arm with a cold wet hand, but she was able to quickly wrest herself free from his grip.

She lunged out of the room. She slammed the bedroom door shut before he could reach her, and shoved her body against the door before he could force it open. Their bodies hit the door simultaneously. She held both palms against the wood and braced her legs outwards, pushing forcefully. The doorknob quietly grated as Brad surreptitiously turned it. Before he could turn it all the way Sara quickly grabbed it, holding it forcefully in place. They both fiercely held the doorknob with a tight grip. The doorknob began to slowly turn. The muscles in her hand burned with constant strain. Minutes passed. The knob began to slide past her grip. She held on until she couldn't fight him any longer. Wrenching it with both hands, he slid the knob past Sara's grip and turned it as far as it would go. She relinquished the knob, focusing instead on holding herself steady against the door. She held both hands against the door and planted both feet on the floor. He pushed hard and she began to slowly slide backwards. She then threw her body against the door and it slammed shut again. The wood pressed against her hands, but she bore the pressure with her feet braced against the floor.

Brad smashed his fist against the door repeatedly with loud thundering knocks of frustration. Her face was pressed against the hard surface. He breathed heavily on the other side. She knew he was stronger. Minutes passed by.

A cord of muscle in her leg began to cramp with electric

pain. She couldn't hold her position. She rolled her shoulder across the door and turned around, locking her back in place against the door. Brad exerted himself mightily against her. She constantly pressed her feet against the floor and pushed her back against the door. The pressure against her back grew as Brad pushed against her. Her calf muscles began to burn with the strain. Several minutes passed. She could feel her legs growing weaker by the moment, and knew that she would not be able to hold herself up indefinitely. Slowly she slid her back downwards against the door. Brad could hear her moving and pushed hard against her, struggling to take advantage of her weakness.

Keeping her body firmly set against the door, holding off Brad's attempts, she slowly slid downwards until she was sitting on the floor with her feet firmly braced. Her wearied legs were given some rest now that she was able to take her weight off of them. She sat with her back flush against the door and her knees towards her chest.

There was nothing within reach. She could see the telephone sitting across the room, so far away it might as well have been at the bottom of the ocean. She could see her purse across the room on the kitchen counter. Her cell phone was inside. It was too far. If she left the door and made a run for it she wouldn't get to it in time. Brad was locked into his position, terrified that if he left the door the sound of his footsteps would betray him, and Sara would have just enough time to race to her cell phone. He had her trapped, but she had him trapped as well. Neither of them had the upper hand. 'He's exhausted from fighting the storm,' Sara said to herself, 'I can outlast him. No matter what he does, I can last longer.'

She could feel him through the door, she thought she could feel his heart beating and his chest rising and falling with every breath, the door pressed between them was simultaneously separating them and connecting them. She felt as if his arms were around her, testing her strength with a ferocious grip.

"You can't hold me like this forever," he said softly, "you know you can't. You're getting tired."

The hard surface pressed against the bones in her back. She couldn't just lean against the door, she had to actively push in order to hold her ground. She kept her knees bent, and her feet constantly pressed against the wooden floor.

"You wouldn't have done that to Joy, would you?" There was silence on the other side of the door. She tried to find a way for Brad to not be the impostor. She wanted to think he was being framed as she had been, but every alibi she could think of fell away as soon as she raised it.

She acerbically recalled a conversation they had on the beach. Brad had seemed so perfect on the surface. His personal philosophy was of following shallow beauty. The reason he was so superficial is that beneath his thin exterior he carried a dark and troubled soul. Just beneath the surface there was a dark and ugly truth that he didn't want to face, and didn't want anyone else to discover. He had to be shallow in order to live with himself.

Hours passed by. He would gently nudge at the door, testing her strength, then lean against it, trying to break through in a moment of Sara's weakness. Sara felt lost in the storm. The storm winds raged outside the house, whistling against every exterior surface. Weakness and strength swung through her body hour by hour. Her world was the storm and the strain until Brad's voice broke through from the other side of the door, "You don't really know this girl that you have been trying to avenge. You've been doing this whole thing over something that you don't understand."

Sara fought against his dark assertions. She had only been pursuing justice from the beginning. "I've been trying to stop a murderer," said Sara coldly, "You're a serial killer. You killed all those people."

"No, I'm not," he admonished, "Are you finally ready to talk about it? I've been waiting on you to calm down."

Sara refused to calm down if that was all he was after. "She didn't just love herself," he continued, "she loved a lot of people apparently. I was just another one of the guys that she was using. That type of girl isn't at peace unless someone is fighting over her."

Sara thought back to her own proclivities. She remembered how she felt as Richard Barrow and Lawrence Dodd had gone to war with each other as they tried to win her heart. In a way, Sara had taught Joy how to use men.

The boiling teapot on the stove finally began whistling a sharp piercing cry. The shrill whistle filled the house as steam spouted.

"The story is more sordid than you know," said Brad, "Bartlett was cheating on Joy with Suzanne. You were right about him," said Brad, without a note of irony. That's why she wanted him dead. She just used me to make that happen."

Sara wanted to believe that it was true, she deeply wanted him to be right, but still she kept her back to him. "Do you know what she told me? She told me that she loved me. She did the same thing to Bartlett, only he had more money so I guess she was going to try to get all she could from him." He was actually trying to blame Joy for what happened, as if he was perfectly innocent.

"Joy was a vampire," he continued, "She fed on relationships like a parasite. She hated him so much for cheating. I've never seen someone like that before. I knew something was wrong then. If she really loved me then she wouldn't have cared who he was in love with."

The whistle of the tea kettle faded out as the boiling water completely evaporated, and the kettle sat empty. Despite her terror, she didn't want to overpower Brad, or trick him, or even have him arrested. Her immediate and overwhelming instinct was to rescue him, irrational though it was, because she loved him. If only she could save him. The impossibility of it and the longing for it clashed in Sara's mind with all the force of the stormy waves. Sara felt closer to Joy Turner than ever before, now knowing what it was like to be seduced. Thinking back on how bitterly she criticized Joy she felt the horror of her present situation all the more deeply.

"Joy used me," said Brad, "led me along like she loved me. Joy lied about love. Lying about love is the marriage of heaven and hell. Anyone who lies about love has lost their right to live, because love is the only thing worth living for." His voice strained sharply as he spoke.

"Just let me out of here, Sara. Please."

Sara wrestled against his words. He was trying to seduce her into giving in, she reminded herself. Everything he was saying must be a lie, a badly constructed lie. It was easy to see through. Joy wouldn't have done that. Maybe she told Brad she loved him. Maybe not. He was striking out with lie after lie, but Sara resolved that her heart would be as steadfast as the door. Joy didn't deserve what happened to her, even if she had damaged him.

"All I have done is try to explain to you who she is," continued Brad, "but you still don't know what she did."

The phone in the kitchen rang. To Sara, it sounded like a choir of angels. Someone was out there, outside, trying to reach her.

It rang again. Brad was silent with anticipation. Sara held steady. The phone rang again and the answering machine picked up. Brad's perky voice spoke up, "Hey, this is Brad, leave a message."

The caller's voice echoed through the house, "Hi, it's Sara. What do you think you're doing?"

Chills ran through her neck.

The woman's voice coming from the answering machine was Sara's very own voice.

"Why are you doing this?" she yelled to the door.

Her voice responded from the answering machine, "You'll see..."

CHAPTER 44

The entire scheme was now apparent.

He got close to his victims, surreptitiously accumulating a vocabulary list of words and phrases that could be used to completely replace a person's social existence. The audio files were uploaded onto Brad's laptop, and could be accessed by simply clicking on them. Whenever the situation called for it, all Brad had to do was scroll and click and he could become his victim. The digital clones lived on betraying them, liquidating all their assets and emptying their bank accounts. He was always such a good listener, letting her go on and on as he recorded every word, quietly compiling a library of phrases that he could eventually use to replace her.

"I was going to be next," said Sara.

"No, you're wrong," replied Sara's voice, "The most important thing is for you to be yourself."

Sara was confounded.

"Think about it." said Sara's voice.

The rain battered the roof with thick heavy drops. The relentless downpour consumed the house. The wind blew sheets of rain against the roof in waves, as ocean waves pounded the house underneath. Water struck the house from all angles.

"I never said that to you. I said it to Joy."

Sara was speechless. Silence hung in the air. She had spoken those words to Joy alone. No one else was with them on the beach. It was just her and Joy, side by side, the last time she saw her alive. The implications were confusing, and if not confusing then disturbing.

Sara was lost in thought, until her voice broke the silence, "I'm sorry this had to happen to you."

The answering machine finally beeped and shut off. "You still don't understand, do you?" asked Brad, "It's all about you, Sara. Joy died because of you."

Sara didn't believe a word he said, yet she desperately wanted to know what he was going to tell her.

CHAPTER 45

On a warm, blue skied day the sun beamed freely on the Bartlett estate, illuminating the manicured green landscaping and almost fluorescent white marble statues. Brad sat at a glass table with a martini in his hand. He wore a bright yellow collared t-shirt and white shorts. Despite the drink in his hand, he was not relaxed. He nervously glanced at both the doorway and the driveway.

The light reflecting off her blonde hair, Joy Turner walked onto the deck framed by the arched glass doorway. Her cheeks were flush with color, Suzanne's blush number five to be exact.

Wearing her tight white sun-dress, she walked past small marble tributes to Greek goddesses and exotic palm trees standing in clay pots. Brad gently rocked the martini glass in his hand.

Joy ran her hand lightly along Brad's shoulders as she passed behind him and then sat down beside him, her hand resting on his leg. "Has he been stealing any more from me lately?" she asked.

Brad cleared his throat, "He just made another withdrawal from your account and deposited it with Suzanne."

"It wasn't enough for him to take me shopping there all the time." She tossed a small recorder onto the table, "Here's some audio. I met with Sara Steinberg today. She was angry."

"Good work," said Brad, taking a sip of his drink.

"You should have enough by now, so you can quit stalling. Are you ready?" she asked.

"What?"

"You're all set to take care of her?"

"I am."

"Good. And when you're done," she added, "throw her body in the ocean. That should take care of it, don't you think?"

"It should," said Brad as he took another sip of his martini to calm his nerves. He clicked off the recorder hidden in his pocket.

"Now you know why I had to do it," said Brad. Thunder echoed through the house.

It was like her life had only been built on fantasies and superstitions that were now in the soberness of reality proven to be wrong. This entire time the mastermind behind the plot was dead from the beginning.

"I was supposed to kill you," said Brad, "but I saved you from her. I saved your life. You are alive right now because I killed her. I am relieved that she is dead. You should be too."

"Why did she want to kill me?"

"She said that if we got rid of Bartlett that you and Barbara would be the first ones to figure out who did it. That's why she wanted to go after you first."

Sara still couldn't fathom why Joy would want her dead. The idea was completely foreign and had never crossed her mind. That may have been the justification that she told Brad, but it wasn't the real reason for Joy's hatred of Sara. Sara wondered what effect it would have on Joy if her relationship with Bartlett had been discovered. But that wouldn't be enough to incite that kind of passion, unless Bartlett still had strong feelings for Sara. Maybe Joy didn't just discover some past relationship, but some hidden desire in Bartlett that he refused to relinquish.

"She seduced me after my falling out with Bartlett. She thought she could use that to control me."

Sara then remembered what Bartlett had told her at their dinner.

"Bartlett told me that Joy had insisted that he not sell any more beach houses."

Brad paused. "She did that to me?" It dawned on him that he had been deceived. "She wanted me trapped here so that she could use me. I don't feel bad for her. Bartlett was right to hate her."

Brad pushed firmly against the door. She pushed back even harder.

"Open up the door, Sara."

Her strength was beginning to wane. Mariana had been right. The killer was the one she desired most. She was all alone, fighting against her love with all her heart.

He was there, on the other side of the door, waiting for her weariness to overtake her.

CHAPTER 46

The standoff continued unabated, every minute of every hour that passed. They were hours that felt like agonizing days.

Sara reflected on the death of Joy, 'She was never who I thought she was. The words she spoke to me as she looked me in the eyes, they weren't any more real than the sound recordings over the phone. What was she? Just a voice, and who was controlling it? A stranger, some distant foreigner I will never meet. None of it was real, it was just someone else's fantasy. It wasn't really Joy that died, it was some scheming, murderous stranger.'

"What did you do to her?" asked Sara.

"She drowned in my hands," said Brad, "She didn't even fight very hard. I'm not guilty, I don't feel any guilt about it. That's the same thing as innocent. I broke in through the back door and hid in the kitchen until she finally walked around the corner. I held on just like you're hanging onto that door. You're killing us right now." Sara was bitterly stung by his words. "I don't remember a whole lot," he continued, "Most of the time it feels like it never happened." He spoke as if he expected Sara to be rooting for him.

A low resonant boom shook through Sara as a massive wave hit against the foundation of the house. The entire structure shuddered underneath her as the lights went out. The darkness completely enveloped her. Another wave pounded against the foundation, shaking the house. Something clanged onto the floor. She was surrounded by the deep reverberations in the house. Pressure from the door against Sara's back began to increase.

Outside the house the telephone poles were wrought from their foundations and pulled into the water, dragging the electric lines down with them like fishing line being dragged into the depths by sinkers.

Brad grunted as he shifted his weight on the other side of the door. He paused before speaking, "I know why this door is still closed. You still don't understand. I still haven't told you why I did it. It wasn't because of what she did to me. I did it because I had to protect you. Maybe it was because I had already done so much for you, when I finally met you, I instantly fell for you. I love you, Sara. That's why I did it. I killed for you."

She suspected that he may be lying. He had been the one that tried to have her imprisoned.

"You made them think I confessed. You wanted anyone accused but yourself."

"I knew you wouldn't be imprisoned forever," he retorted, "Barbara would find a way to set you free. Can you blame me? You are very dangerous when you want something."

She knew he was referencing her pursuit of Bartlett. "Don't pretend like you didn't want me to go after him," said Sara, disgusted.

"I just wanted to keep you busy, I didn't think you would actually be able to imprison an innocent man, but I underestimated you. You are very good at getting what you want, no matter if it's true or not. So I guess the guilty ones don't stand a chance."

"And why Suzanne? Why did you do it?"

"She was goading Bartlett into having you convicted. That wasn't hard to see. She was probably worried that the finger would get pointed at him eventually. I had already killed for you once. I didn't want that to be for nothing."

Sara thought he was lying, that he actually hated Bartlett and wanted him dead. He killed Suzanne in order to bring Bartlett's world crashing around him and isolate him so that when he killed Bartlett he would be able to move into his house and replace him without arousing suspicion. Maybe that is what Brad wanted all along. That was why he cheated with Joy, to get even with Bartlett.

Sara thought back on her relationship with Brad. Everything took a new slant, the stories she told him, and the questions he asked. The efforts to barricade his house from the storm took on a more desperate edge. He had to have the house so that he could lose himself in the ocean everyday.

"I will let you go if you let me out of here," he said, "You can run outside and I won't follow you, you know that I won't let this house be torn apart. I'll even back away from the door. Can you hear me?" His voice sounded more distant and the creaking of his footsteps receded. "You don't have to trust me," he called out, "I'm going to give you a head start."

He listened for the sound of her rising to her feet but she remained fixed in place. She had only a second to brace herself as she heard the floorboards rapidly creaking on the other side of the door. He ran as fast as he could on his exhausted legs and slammed his weight into the rock solid door. The door latch shattered the wood holding it back.

The door lunged forward eight inches, her body sliding against the hard wood floor. The shock wave tingled Sara's spine and she could hear his low groan as he stood leaning against the doorway with a deeply bruised shoulder. The door slammed shut again as she pushed back.

His voice was weighted with a heavy tone and a hard edge, "They think that you murdered Joy. If you turn on me I'll have to turn on you. Don't make me do that. I can protect you. Just back away from the door. I saved your life before, I can save you again."

Now he had turned on her and revealed himself. He was trying to take her by force, offering to protect her from himself.

She didn't say a word to him. Her silence was the response to his threat. She rubbed her sore thigh, and pressed her feet against the floor even harder. An hour passed by in silence between them as thunder rumbled and the ocean pounded around them. Sweat ran down her forehead and dripped from the ends of her hair.

Despite all the listening he had done, he didn't really understand what she had told him. 'He should have known,' she thought to herself, 'that even joy deserved justice.' He must have been incapable of understanding it.

"She's not a murderer Brad, you are. It does not matter if Joy wasn't worth fighting for. I'm not fighting for her, I'm fighting for me. Killing her wasn't worth it, because I don't love you. I never knew who you were. Everything you said to me or did for me was a lie. Barbara is going to come looking for me eventually. Otherwise, I'm going to hold you here until the end. The ocean is going to have to drag me away from this door."

The desperate anticipation was broken by the loud ring of the telephone. Sara stared across the room at the phone as it rang again over the pounding of the storm. The phone rang out a third time and, fearing that Brad would try to take advantage of the distraction, Sara braced her back hard against the door. The answering machine clicked on. Brad's voice was upbeat: "Hey, this is Brad, leave a message."

"Sara, are you there?" There was no sound more welcome, the voice on the answering machine was Barbara's. If only she could reach that phone. She was only a few feet away from salvation. As Sara desperately searched again for some way to reach the phone Barbara continued to speak, "Honey, you should have listened to me."

But something didn't seem quite right in her tone. "You'll save yourself a lot of trouble if you turn yourself in right now," Barbara said.

Now that she was critically analyzing Barbara's voice she could tell that something was wrong.

"Hey, honey," said Barbara, "What are you doing? You'd better cut that out." Sara realized the implications.

"Isn't he cute," said Barbara's voice.

"You're right," said Brad, confirming her worst fears, "That's not her."

CHAPTER 47

Sara could hear the sound of sand sliding away underneath the floorboards. The ocean had breached the fortress wall, and the sand foundation below was steadily eroding away.

"Listen," said Brad, "Barbara is still alive. I tied her up in her basement. The water is probably pouring in there right now." Every word he spoke was full of horror.

Barbara was completely alone, like Sara, with no one to protect her from being swallowed alive. 'If only Barbara could get free, slip off those ropes, then she could fight her way through the storm and find me, and rescue me like she has so many times in the past,' Sara thought to herself, but this was not like those years gone by. Sara was acutely aware that it was she who had to save herself and rescue them both.

Brad continued, "If you leave right now you can get there before the water does." Sara didn't respond. She was frozen in place, unable to move an inch. She wanted to run for it and either reach the front door or her phone, but she knew that Brad would overtake her if he had the chance. Her anguish swelled. Minutes passed.

"Are you going to let her die?"

Sara was lost in intense pensive thought.

Brad wanted her to do something reckless, she told herself. She tried in vain to avoid visualizing Barbara, trapped and helpless, the water inching up her body, no one around to rescue her.

"She's probably thinking about you, Sara."

Sara wanted to break through the door and throttle Brad. She knew exactly what Barbara would say, she would tell her to hold her ground and not give in to him like he wanted. Sara wouldn't allow him to use Barbara and get the better of her. 'Maybe he is lying,' Sara told herself, 'or maybe Barbara escaped.' She didn't believe that to be true, but it could be true, it was enough to give her the strength to hold her ground. Minutes more passed.

This explosive new persona revealed to Sara that he had truly been an impostor all along. The man who steadfastly awaited the assault of the coming storm had now disappeared and in his place a primal ranting fiend had been revealed. He was a monster. He only acts like an animal, she thought to herself, because he is caged. He has become what he was forced to be. He is desperate because he has had everything pulled away from him. He pleads because so little has been given to him. He is explosive because he has been so tightly confined. He had become so twisted by the turns in his life that he lost sight of reality.

She wanted to be able to reach out and grab Barbara's hand.

"It's too late," Brad groaned, "It's over her head by now, Sara. You killed her. Your stubbornness will kill you too. I know it's eating away at you. You're going to remember this forever, and you're going to regret what you did."

The sea outside roared.

"Are you scared of dying here tonight?" asked Brad.

He had used both flattery and nightmares against her, and still she would not relent. He began beating the back of his head against the door.

A long drawn out cracking filled Sara's ears as the deck slowly broke off of the house and collapsed into the surf below. The long beams of the deck began slamming against the barricade wall like a hundred battering rams striking simultaneously with each rhythmic swell of the forceful water. Brad screamed, "Let me out of here, I've got to fix this house! It's being torn apart!"

The beams below continued ramming into the house.

"You're murdering the both of us!"

"I wouldn't kill you Brad, I'm nothing like you."

The support beams under the house groaned against the ceaseless assault of the ocean swells as Sara held the door firm and ached against the constant pressure behind it.

She was deafened by the clamor of a wild force of nature battering the structure around her. The deep beating of the ocean felt like an earthquake jarring the entire structure from its base. The entire house shuddered and abruptly shifted to one side. Sara held on, keeping herself pressed against the door. As the house abruptly shook again Brad was able to force the door forward a few inches.

He thrust his hand through the opening and grasped wildly. He managed to grab a handful of her hair. He gripped it fiercely and pulled backwards before she could close the door. The door slammed shut again as her head hit against the doorway. She was tied to the door now by her long black hair, her neck bent to the side. Brad wrapped the black locks around his fist so that they would not come loose. Sara tried to pull her head forward, but the roots of her hair held tight. She held her body against the door, and Brad pulled against her equally as hard. "If you let me go then I will let you go," he said. She strained her head slightly forward but Brad yanked harshly and the back of her head hit against the door.

She breathed hard and fast. Minutes passed. Gathering her strength, she pulled forward, allowing the door to partially open. His hand was quickly jerked into the doorway. She then flung back against the door and pushed hard, smashing his hand. Brad cried out. His fingers contorted and his scream bellowed. Her hair slipped from his fingers. He threw his body against the door again, but was only able to move the door far enough to allow him to withdraw his battered hand.

The floor beneath Sara rumbled. The foundation had fractured. She could feel it as acutely as she could feel her own heart breaking.

CHAPTER 48

She was frozen and terrified. Darkness surrounded her. She could only imagine her death, and was powerless to stop it. Brad would overtake her, or the storm would seize and crush her. In her dark confusion she could only see one faint light. It appeared when she thought of Barbara. She felt like Mariana, listening for an ethereal voice to guide her.

As the foundation shook, a rift in the ceiling opened up with the loud cracking of shattering boards. Broken debris rained down as the center of the roof collapsed. The largest beams missed Sara, crashing beside her. She was pelted by splinters and wind as a gaping expanse opened above and a rough slab of the roof was ripped downwards. Bright blue flashes of lightning illuminated Sara and her surroundings. The doorway was still intact. She wiped the shards of wood away from her hair. A pile of wreckage had landed not far from Sara. There were cracked shingles and boards with bent nails sticking out of them. Water began pouring into the middle of the house through the wide hole in the open roof. Sara could almost hear Barbara telling her what to do. She eyed the pile of debris that had fallen in. She reached out with her foot and gingerly pulled the cracked two-by-four from the wreckage, sliding it across the wet floor, careful to be quiet. She could hear Brad breathing on the other side of the door. Finally the board was close enough to grab. The tips of her fingers barely reached the top edge of the two-by-four. She pressed down on the board and ever so slightly slid it toward her. Now that it was in reach she was able to silently lift it off the floor by one end. It wobbled in her unsteady hand and the other end began to tilt towards the floor, but she strained and regained her balance and brought it back upright and drew it closer. She moved quietly, careful to not make a sound as she lifted the board into the air and carefully moved it towards the door.

She slowly slid the top of the two-by-four underneath the doorknob and held it there firmly, then drew a deep breath and placed the bottom of the two-by-four on the floor, being careful not to make the slightest tap. The board was still only loosely in place, and would slip away at the slightest jar. The rain poured over her matted hair. She brushed a heavy strand of hair away from her eye, then gently pushed her weight against the board, forcing it securely against the door, and so turned part of Brad's barricade into her own. Carefully, she slowly slid away from the door, the sound of her movement masked by the splashes of rain. Bracing her hand against her knee, she quietly pushed herself to her feet. Her eyes stayed constantly fixed to the doorway. She anticipated throwing herself at the door at any moment. The cell phone was only two steps away.

She silently took a step backwards, and apprehensively reached behind her towards the phone. She grasped only at air. She took another step back and reached again, and felt the familiar contours of her cell phone. Rain poured down over Sara's hair and face from the gaping hole in the roof. She held

218

down on the power button of the cell phone and held it in front of her and waited for it to light up, her eyes still focused on the door.

Behind Sara, illuminated by sudden rapid flashes of lightning, two legs descended from the open ceiling. Sara's cell phone finally lit up. Thunder rumbled through the house.

CHAPTER 49

Brad's dripping wet feet hit the floor behind her as he dropped down from the roof above. Sara's scream of terror drowned out the clamor of the storm. He seized her with both hands firmly gripping her shoulders. He squeezed, and pulled her towards him, and as he did Sara grabbed the two-by-four braced against the door and pulled it loose, then swung it around and slammed it against Brad's head. It seemed to happen instantaneously, his body falling backwards in unconsciousness and hitting the wreckage strewn floor, and the floorboards cracking under the sudden weight and snapping. The floor of the house shattered around him in a jagged crevasse and he fell below and splashed into the darkness.

He seemed to disappear in slow motion as the water completely covered him. She was stunned by the impact, and the board dropped from her hands. She had not been trying to kill him. She did not want him dead.

Her mind was a storm in the critical moment between watching him fall unconscious into the murky wreck and bracing her hands in front of her and diving in after him. As she watched him fall she felt compelled to fall with him, as if they were both tethered by a line.

In a tremendous rush of wreckage his body plunged inside, as if he were swallowed whole by a whale's mouth. The deep round cavern was full of debris. The salty ocean water battered his body and flooded into his lungs.

She recognized that down in the dark unknown there lay her chance to finally rescue Brad, if not spiritually then physically.

She dove into the debris-filled raging water, risking her life for the murderer. She realized, after she jumped, that Barbara, wherever she was, would never forgive her.

She splashed into the rough water. Splintered boards forcefully swirled in the deadly brew. She swept her arms through the dark water trying to find him. She then dove, disappearing into the rough froth.

Boards scraped past her and tugged at her clothes as she moved. She emerged from the black water with her hair over her face and her arm tightly wrapped around Brad's chest.

In the rapid intermittent flashes of lightning Sara looked around at the wreckage strewn water. With one arm she pushed a panel of soaked drywall aside and pulled out a splintered two-by-eight and pushed it out of the churning chasm to form a ramp. Finding her footing on some jagged pieces of timber, she pushed upwards and lifted Brad's weight towards the ramp.

She pulled him up the ramp inch by inch, dragging his dripping body with all of her strength, refusing to let go. She clenched her fists around his shirt as tight as she could. Laboriously she surmounted the ramp and pulled him over the edge. His mouth hung agape and his head was laying to one side. His salvaged frame laid silently upon the floor. Blood ran down his arms from deep cuts.

She laid a hand on each cheek and pressed her face to his. She parted those lips she had kissed before and pressed her lips against them and breathed all of her air from her lungs into his. His chest rose and fell. As she rose for a breath she looked down at his face. It remained cold and unresponsive. She breathed deeply into his mouth again as all of the warm rich air flowed out of her body. As she began to inhale she felt cold fingers closing around her throat. Her lips were still locked against his, and she found herself unable to breathe and struggled against him face to face as his eyes shot open.

CHAPTER 50

Her chest strained to suck in air, but her throat was closed. Her last breath had been the one that gave him life. She clenched her teeth and bit his lips, she could taste the blood on her tongue. She felt herself going faint. He pressed his fingers into her until she stopped choking. Her eyes stared into nothing. Her collapsed body fell on top of him. He released her neck and pushed her limp body aside. He got to his feet and walked through the wreckage in the kitchen and began furiously picking up boards and throwing them aside. He then thrust his bloody hand down into the debris and lifted up his claw hammer. When he turned back to where he had left Sara she was nowhere to be seen.

Sara stood on the edge of the house facing the roiling ocean. It hadn't been the first time she had to fake her death. She looked out at the expanse of water. The house was an island in the storm, with rough water all around. The raindrops flew sideways on the swift wind, hitting her skin like needles.

As she squinted she could barely make out an object

bobbing on the rough sea. She wiped the rainwater from her eyes. It was a sailboat being tossed about. She recognized it at once, the stranded sailboat had been lifted from the beach's grasp by the storm flood, and was knocking around on the waves, the sails clapping forcefully in the wind.

She jumped into the water immediately and began swimming towards the boat. Pieces of hard unseen debris snagged at her legs as she swam. The flashes of lightning illuminated the rocking sailboat. She swam past floating beams which threatened to force her under as the ocean worked them like levers. The boat sat low in the water, fighting to keep afloat. A loose wet rope whipped around and Sara was able to grab hold of it as the sailboat bucked wildly on the waves. She pulled herself up the side. The seawater sloshed around as Sara climbed in. Most of the canvas sails were torn, but the main sail had been folded down and secured, so Sara cut it loose. The storm winds caught it and forcefully tried to punch through it, but the sail held steady. Sara grabbed the mainsail and aimed the cutter down the beach.

As the boat trudged over the rough waves the house behind Sara finally collapsed in on itself. Walls bent and crumpled, boards cracked and collapsed. The piled mountain of wet interlocking timbers formed a primal cage that gripped Brad tight as he cried out.

She steered the speeding boat over cresting waves and sharp wreckage, and through the darkness headed straight for Barbara's house.

CHAPTER 51

The sun had broken over the horizon and the downpour had abated, but the heavy clouds still covered the sky overhead, only allowing a dim glow through to the storm-swept land below.

Sara hoped that the swells of water had spared Barbara's neighborhood entirely, but with each passing demolished home her hope diminished. As she neared her destination only the landscape looked familiar, the homes were unrecognizable. Roofs had been lifted off their crumpled walls and broken into shards. Halves of houses had been gripped by the ocean and pulled into the depths. Mats of drywall were laid upon the sidewalks and heaps of boards were on the streets. Mud and sand were mixed with pieces of fine furniture and dishes. Amongst the wreckage she could make out the half-collapsed home of Barbara's neighbor. Sara turned the boat and headed towards the shore, then leapt from the boat as it entered the shallows.

She held her footing as she walked through uneven and wobbly wreckage which caught her feet with each step.

Though her legs were exhausted she ran across the tangles of wood and mounds of debris until she finally arrived at the spot where Barbara's house should have been. Small pools of murky water stood surrounded by blocks of concrete and warped metal pipes.

There was nothing left standing. It had all fallen and been lost. It was almost beautiful in a way, how the entire house had been swept away. Sara expected to see Barbara tired but healthy, resting on a piece of debris. Sara felt a strain in her throat.

Barbara hadn't gone easily. It took an entire ocean to take her life. Sara remembered Barbara's old saying about relationships, 'You measure sadness by tears, you measure love by sacrifice.' Her mind drifted back to the first time she met Barbara, when she had raven black hair and a smoldering gaze that was indomitable.

Sara thought back to Barbara's motherly advice and admonitions, her reassurances when the future seemed bleak, her insight when the mysteries seemed impenetrable, and a faith that tomorrow would be no more difficult than today. The destruction was as devastatingly complete as Sara's heartbreak. She wouldn't still be alive if it hadn't been for everything Barbara had taught her. She wouldn't have had the will to hold back the door against the raving murderer if it hadn't been for Barbara's unyielding example. She could picture Barbara with crystal clarity, the images flashed through her mind, and all of them were from happier times. Barbara's silver gown on inauguration day glittered vibrantly. Her steely eyes glimmered in the chaotic circus ring. Reflections of fireworks sparkled off her diamonds. There was no one more beautiful, and no one that Sara loved more. The tears fell from her eyes onto the flooded ground. The great absence of her friend fully hit her. It was the end of a way of life, because Barbara was a part of so many aspects of her life, and the full ramifications of it couldn't be imagined.

She stood alone in a field of tangled wreckage, and stared out forlornly over the ocean. Unbeknownst to her the Judge stepped from behind a mountain of debris behind her, precariously walking over puddles and broken boards as he carried Barbara snugly in his arms. Her head laid limply across his arm, her grey hair dangled in the soft wind, and her eyelids were closed. He walked to a dry board that was resting on the ground like a bench. He laid her limp body down, carefully lowering her head with his hands, and then sat down beside her. Tears fell onto Sara's cheeks as she heard the creaking of the boards and turned to see Barbara laying beside the Judge.

"She needs some mouth-to-mouth."

"I think she's already breathing," said Sara. Disregarding her, the Judge hurriedly pried Barbara's mouth open and put his mouth against hers and exhaled deeply, at the exact same instant that Barbara's hand came across and smacked him in the face. "Blah," said Barbara, "now I've got the Judge taste in my mouth."

Tendrils of grey hair were draped across her face, but she ran her fingers through her hair twice over, and it fell into line and assumed its normal posture.

"Can you get me some banana pudding from the fridge?"

The Judge leaned over and opened the door to a refrigerator which was half-buried in the mud. He reached inside and pulled out a large glass bowl full of creamy yellow banana pudding.

Barbara looked around and surveyed the destruction around her.

"I don't want to believe it," said Barbara.

"Your living room," said Sara.

A fractured leg from an antique table jutted out of the ground. The formerly pristine carpet was now torn and caked with thick silt. Decorative plates which had formerly been delicately positioned for display were now broken into shards and scattered all over. Figurines of rabbits and cats were mixed in with broken boards and dry-wall, and the vacuum cleaner was half-buried in the mud.

"Sara. Don't stand on the carpet," said Barbara wearily. Sara looked down and then stepped to the side.

Bright beams of golden light finally broke through the distant clouds. Barbara's home was in ruins, but her spirit was still standing strong. She shrugged, "That's what bank accounts are for."

Sara turned to the Judge, "Have you got your cell phone?"

"Um, sure," he said, reaching into his pocket.

"I need to call the police."

Several policemen were already at the scene as Sara, Barbara, and the Judge arrived. The officers climbed over the jagged pile of shattered boards which had formerly been Brad's fortress. The moat was now filled in with silt, and boards jutted out at all angles. Sara followed after the officers and climbed through the remnants of the barricade wall. The detective was on his knees, pushing boards aside. Several of the beams were laid over the remnants of the kitchen. Sara pulled board after board off the pile until her hand touched flesh. "He's alive."

Sara and Barbara stood on a sandy bank and watched as the policemen pried Brad's semi-conscious body from the splintered wreckage and brought him into custody. His wrists were bound with handcuffs and his grim stare spoke of betrayal, as his dreams had been betrayed by the wrath of nature, and by the unsuspecting girl at the beach.

The detective approached Sara, managing a smile, "You managed to get away from the police when the storm hit. I sent them to protect you," he admonished. Sara, though she was tired, laughed.

Before heading to a hotel, at Barbara's behest, sopping wet, the three of them, they walked up and down Barbara's devastated neighborhood picking up brightly colored high-heels as they found them scattered about in gutters, underneath sagging rooftops, and hanging precariously on tree branches.

Sara laid in bed that night trying to fall asleep, and as the faltering storm winds rattled the windows with remnants of rainfall she tried to imagine what violent fantasies must run through Brad's mind as he sits in that cramped prison cell. He probably dreams of water, it slowly boils and rises from the beach, the entire horizon swells, the water follows the dark clouds into the city, rushing through the streets and turning over cars, invading quiet homes, rushing over those caught unaware, strangling those who he would have strangled, and finally the violent flood crashes into the prison walls, eating away at the foundation, tearing at the razor wire and crumbling walls, and he leaps from his cell into the familiar stormy surge, and is held fast by the ocean's strong current as he floats miles away, drifting peacefully towards paradise.

CHAPTER 52

The newspaper article detailed the entire ghastly scheme. The murdering of the innocent victims and using their own voice to fill the empty shell left behind, closing all bank accounts, breaking personal relationships to delay suspicion, and once the serial killer had insinuated himself fully into their lives, to sell the empty house itself, squeezing every last coin from the victim. He was, they say, planning to move from house to house as his greedy ambition and murderous aloofness grew with each new acquisition, and so the press labeled him the 'Hermit Crab.'

Sara folded the newspaper and handed it back to the old woman sitting on the green bench. "Thanks," said Sara. "Hrmph," the woman replied.

But Sara wasn't completely exonerated. She made the decision to let Joy's parents go on thinking that she was a bad person, because that's what a good person she was. They would be able to hold onto a fond memory of their innocent daughter Joy that would surely comfort them in the years to come.

Sara walked down the empty sidewalk past stores that were still boarded up, except for one, the Beauty Queen Dress Shop. 'It's a shame,' Sara thought, 'that Suzanne had to die like that.' The 'Beauty Queen Dress Shop' was now under the management of a new beauty queen, Suzanne's assistant James. As she passed the shop window admiring the new lines of men's and women's dresses, she noticed a new beauty product being advertised. The label on the bottle read, "Ocean Mist: for fuller body," and showed a picture of a woman with luxurious black hair emerging from the water with a sultry smirk on her face. The sign in front read: 'The fairest way to measure a woman's beauty is by her hair,' a quote taken directly from Barbara. Sara cursed herself, 'I knew I should have made that.'

"We could have made another fortune," said Barbara. Barbara was standing right behind Sara. Her silver hair positively glowed in the sunlight. "Let's get something to eat," she said with a smile, "Everybody's at the grill."

The whirlwind survivors were now shooting the breeze in the weary celebratory atmosphere at Wiley's oyster bar and grill. They gathered together to relate their ordeals to one another, glad-handing and consoling at once. Drinks were on the house, and to the harried patrons the beverages were worth their weight in gold. Everyone in the restaurant had one hand on a cold glass, including Sara and Barbara with their margaritas.

The melodic clangs of the steel drum band played along with the conversations of the storm survivors. A young Hispanic girl danced beside them swinging her hips and shaking a maraca that looked just like Sara's old cell phone.

The locals considered it an act of divine justice that king Neptune had spared the restaurant. The seafood, they said, was judged to be a worthy sacrifice.

At the next table over, Jay Wiley, the owner of the restaurant, was telling his favorite story about how Sara and Barbara had helped him recover his precious pearl, and about how painful it had been to auction off such a beautiful jewel. "It doesn't matter after all, two pearls are better than one," he said as he patted Sara and Barbara on their backs.

The towering palms held the evening glow as pointed palm fronds rustled with the warm ocean breeze. The ocean had calmed into tranquility as if it had exhausted itself with its tempestuous storm and was now laying supine, ashamed of its transgressions. The tanned young ten-year-old girl danced rhythmically from side to side as she shook her noisy cell phone maraca to the Caribbean beat.

Sara had been holding back from Barbara, not telling her every detail about that stormy night. She was almost too ashamed to tell her, but she knew that she must. "I haven't told you something about that night. I did something before I came to find you. Brad had fallen into the water, he was gone, and I could have left and tried to find you, but I didn't. I knew he wanted to kill me and I jumped in and saved him anyway." "You don't have to be ashamed of that," said Barbara reassuringly, "You jumped in because you obviously weren't afraid of him. Part of you knew that I could take care of myself. Sometimes you assume the worst in yourself." 'Perhaps,' Sara thought, 'Barbara was right yet again.'
Sara then heard some familiar mutterings behind her. Mariana came sauntering up, winding her way around tables and having one half of a conversation with her cell phone. "There you are," said Barbara, "Where have you been?"
Mariana took a seat beside them. She looked relaxed, as usual.
"I had a premonition that the country club would be safe from the storm so I waited it out there."
"So they made it out alright?" asked Barbara.

"All the exercise equipment got flooded-" "That's a shame."
"-but other than that everything is fine. I may have put a few things on your tab," Mariana added.

"Don't worry about it," said Barbara.

"I'm glad things went smoothly for you," said Sara, sarcastically.

"You know," said Mariana, "these spirits, they keep telling me to do a reading for you. I don't know why, but they won't leave me alone about it. Hold still for just a second."

Sara looked over at Barbara, who looked back expectantly. Then Sara shrugged and let Mariana stare into her eyes. Mariana placed her ring-covered fingers along either side of Sara's face. Then she reached down and took hold of Sara's hand and ran her fingers across the lines on her palm. "That is strange," she said with a genuine note of surprise, "You are still in love with him." She looked into Sara's eyes, probing deeper for the hidden and mysterious motives that would guide future events. "But you won't be for long," she added, "You will get over him, like you always do." She took hold of Sara's arm, "You are a strong girl," and then she turned and said to Barbara, "You could learn something from her. Try and do that while I'm gone."

"You're going?" asked Barbara.

"Destiny called me," said Mariana, "She's going back to jail so I have to take care of her kids."

"Good luck with that," said Sara.

"It's inevitable, child. Destiny is a damn fool. Anyway, I made a little money on the side helping people out around town. It's more than enough to pay you back for your kindness. Here's some for you as well, Sara." She pulled several hundred dollar bills from her purse and handed them to Sara and Barbara. "You know what you need, Sara? Hope." Mariana then added, "She gives the best massages, tell her I sent you."

Mariana started to leave, but then hesitated, "Oh, Sara, your mother says to tell you that your work isn't done, whatever that is supposed to mean."

Sara and Barbara exchanged glances. Mariana smiled with her wide spaced teeth and then turned as if distracted by some new spirit and walked out of the restaurant whispering to herself as she went.

"I've always enjoyed laying out at the beach as the sun sets," said Barbara, changing the subject. Sara didn't reply, but only looked out over the ocean. They sat down in a couple of beach chairs facing the sea, with plates of Wiley's fresh crabs beside them.

"Saying that you have bad luck with men is becoming an understatement," said Barbara, "I want you to think for a moment, honey. You spent all that time trying to warn Joy about her fiancé, and then look who you wound up with."

Out over the ocean pieces of wreckage from the storm drifted by amongst the pink reflections of the setting sun. One piece of wreckage in particular looked familiar. Sara squinted and could make out her small green car bobbing along with the waves, heading towards the horizon.

"I'll get you a new one," said Barbara.

"That would be nice," replied Sara. It reminded Sara about Barbara's demolished home. "What about you, what about your house? Maybe you could stay with me for a while."

"I wouldn't want to impose," said Barbara.

"I wouldn't mind," replied Sara, "It will be like the old days."

"I was kind of afraid of that," answered Barbara, "Well, I might not be around all the time, though. I've started seeing him again." Barbara pulled a small, polished wooden gavel out of her purse and tapped it against a thick crab claw.

The ocean seemed wider, farther, and deeper than ever. Sunlight shimmered across the entire surface brilliantly.

"Look at that sunset," declared Barbara, "it looks like God opened up a treasure chest."

The two girls at the beach sipped on their margaritas and enjoyed the peaceful beachfront view.

ABOUT THE AUTHOR

Brett Farkas is the author of several books, including:
The Magic Farmer
The Bible II: Paradise Omnipresent

Follow Brett Farkas on twitter for
updates on new releases:
@BrettFarkas

The adventures of Sara
and Barbara will continue.

33011130R00151

Made in the USA
Middletown, DE
27 June 2016